FATAL MEDICINE

FATAL MEDICINE

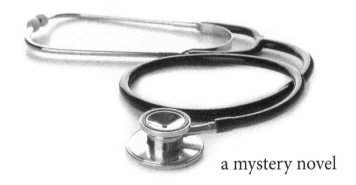

a mystery novel

Henry Averns

Published in 2024 by
Kinetics Design, KDbooks.ca

Published in 2024 by Kinetics Design, KDbooks.ca

ISBN 978-1-998351-00-8 (paperback)

ISBN 978-1-998351-01-5 (ebook)

Edited by Michael Carroll

Cover and interior design, typesetting, online publishing, and printing by Daniel Crack, Kinetics Design, KDbooks.ca
www.linkedin.com/in/kdbooks

Front cover:
Shutterstock 377556520. Closeup of blood, photo contributor, conzorb
Shutterstock 1060370513. Medical stethoscope, photo contributor, Pixel-Shot

Back Cover:
Shutterstock 132379220. Bloodstains, photo contributor, Oksana Mizina

Page 2:
Shutterstock 132379220. Bloodstains, photo contributor, Oksana Mizina

Page 3:
Shutterstock 1060370513. Medical stethoscope, photo contributor, Pixel-Shot

Page 6:
Shutterstock 286394432. Kitchen knife dripping in blood, photo contributor, sharps

Dedicated to my unscrupulous colleagues past and present, without whom there would be no inspiration. And to the colleagues with integrity who represent beacons of hope in the profession.

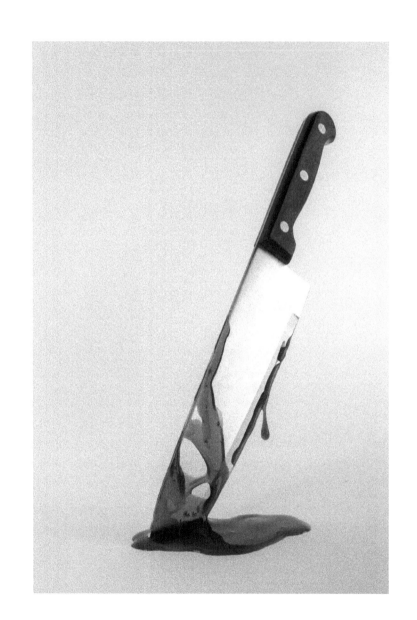

Contents

Prologue

It was a beautiful cottage backing onto fields on the edge of the Forest of Dean — a small stone home with wisteria growing around the front door. Cheryl Bennett had bought it on impulse with her inheritance three years earlier, picturing herself living in a rural idyll. However, her work was eighty miles away, and having made the cottage the perfect getaway, she ended up turning it into a holiday rental. It was changeover day. The last tenant had rented at the very last minute and agreed to leave the £1,500 in cash in the kitchen. It was always good to avoid paying tax.

The cleaning fee covered the basics: sheets, bathroom, floors, et cetera. Anything more extensive would come out of the deposit, but because this was a cash deal, that wouldn't be happening. A liquefying corpse on the sofa was going to be relatively complex to deal with, and perhaps the next guests, arriving in three hours, should be delayed.

The corpse was undoubtedly that of a male, probably in his sixties, wearing only a pair of boxers with a rainbow logo over the crotch. He had curly grey hair, too much for a sixty-year-old, and a rather smug facial expression even in death and recent decay. The man had kept the place remarkably clean, she acknowledged; indeed, the bed was made and all the crockery put away. There was no money in the bread bin. Bastard. More oddly, there was no suitcase and no other clothing. For a moment, Cheryl, ever practical, considered moving the corpse. Perhaps she could drag it out to the shed so that when the police came the cottage would still be rentable. She thought about tossing a throw over the stained sofa and renting the place for another week. But in the absence of an available blanket, she called the police. She remained on the phone for thirty minutes and eventually spoke to an Inspector McAlister, who despite not being there in person felt there was no sign of foul play. Since there was a soccer semifinal live on television, the police delayed their arrival until six in the evening.

Cheryl wondered, when the week's renters arrived, excited to be escaping the city for a week, if telling them there was going to be a few hours' delay owing to a cadaver in the living room would put them off. She hoped not. Cheryl needed the money to pay for a new exhaust on her car. When the police did arrive, there was little enthusiasm from Inspector McAlister to investigate, so the body was taken away in a black van for postmortem examination the following week.

Later the following Monday, the pathologist carried out a full post-mortem. Full in the vaguest meaning of the word, since "attention to detail" wasn't a phrase commonly applied to him.

Cause of death: widespread metastatic carcinoma, with a primary in the colon. Other than the fact that the corpse had rented the holiday cottage for two weeks and seemed to have been dead since arriving, the pathologist noted no other findings other than two balls of cotton wool in the rectum, which weren't even mentioned in the report. No foul play. No toxins. No trauma.

Nobody involved had any imagination. There was an air of apathy over the whole incident, which, of course, suited Cheryl, since she needed to get more renters in as soon as possible. She bought a National Trust tartan blanket to cover the stain, doused it liberally with eau de toilette, and life went on as before.

The coroner recorded a verdict of death by natural causes in an unknown male, and in the absence of a crime, or anybody to claim the body, the corpse was cremated two weeks later.

1

Introducing Myself

My name is Brian Standish. I became a distinctly average hematologist, but I've always wished myself to be a gifted author. Although from my first English homework at the age of seven until my last attempt at getting an article published, this talent has apparently been less obvious to others. Throughout many years working in a hospital laboratory waiting for assays taking four hours at a time, I developed storylines for many excellent novels, none of which I completed. In addition, I began to write a "Guide to Parenting" and a children's book series about a mysterious villain called Kathmandu who never prevailed with his wicked plans. I abandoned this when my wife told me that sex scenes in a book aimed at five-year-olds might not have widespread appeal.

One particularly dull day, I had a further inspired moment of genius when I realized I could develop some "Rules of Medicine" to guide medical students and indeed all health-care professionals.

Somehow life took over. I married Catherine, had children, and all my projects that would have enlightened the world were put on hold. In fact, my novel *Meat*, which had been entirely saved on a floppy disk — all two thousand words of it — remains lost to mankind, since I accidentally threw out all my disks when they became obsolete.

The book was to be written in the style of Alistair MacLean. I still remember the first paragraph: "It was hot. Damn hot. In the distance, a dog barked. Chet Steel sat at the laboratory bench plotting revenge on the journal reviewers who had rejected his latest paper."

My wife told me she felt it was unlikely that a dog would bark in a lab and that calling the hero Chet Steel was a little ridiculous, but she acknowledged I understood the formula needed to write a successful novel, and a rejected academic paper was certainly original.

The book focused on the disenfranchised Chet, who was able to biopsy his own quadriceps muscle and grow the muscle cells in a laboratory, ultimately making enough to form burgers, which he fed to reviewers. The specific details, with hindsight, might have stretched credulity, though having spent two years growing cell lines in petri dishes, I could see that was clearly possible.

Somewhere there's a landfill where a floppy disk lies that might have made my future and would, of course, become a great movie. Such is the capricious nature of fate. Instead, I completed my postgraduate medical training and became a hematologist at Kilminster General Hospital, a small regional hospital in the west of England.

Recently, I met Laura Haythornthwaite again, an almost-previous girlfriend, who suggested I document the terrible events at Kilminster in the 1990s. I'd nearly slept with Laura, and if I had, perhaps my gifts would have been available many years earlier. We'd almost had carnal knowledge on a Thursday evening after finishing a bottle of Blue Nun wine and Pot Noodles while watching *Top of the Pops* in our student accommodation. My three housemates had gone to the cinema that night, but I was keen to save my money, since I wanted to purchase an Airfix model of a Spitfire the coming weekend.

While the precise events leading up to the moment are vague in my memory, I specifically recall Laura removing her jeans and top and standing in front of me. I was irritated because I was watching Mike Oldfield perform "Tubular Bells." Her white bra had been washed with colours, something one should never do, and was a little grey and frayed. But the issue was her underwear. They clearly said "Monday" on the crotch, and today was Thursday. It was like finding a piece of fillet steak that had accidentally been left out for three days. No one would want to risk food poisoning.

And thus, she and I didn't become a couple.

When I met Laura many years later, shopping in Marks and Spencer and wearing a navy quilted gilet, she was delighted to reminisce about my previous novels, none completed. I noticed in her basket there were some days-of-the-week knickers as well as a box of mini-pork pies from the food hall. I was backed up against the reinforced bras as she excitedly urged me to take up my pen again, and feeling a little vulnerable, I agreed. And so I did.

Of course, I've avoided clichés, but be prepared for a roller-coaster ride, since truth is stranger than fiction.

2

Ginger Nuts and Coffee

Not long before I took up my post of consultant hematologist at Kilminster General Hospital, my predecessor, Alisha Sharma, had stormed off, never to be seen again after a particularly unpleasant row with the chief executive officer over three patient deaths from atypical pneumonia. The managers had told her that her mortality rates would flag the hospital if they got any worse. She responded that if patients were infected with the HIV virus when receiving blood products, the hospital targets were hardly relevant. Alisha then received written and verbal warnings that such talk wouldn't be tolerated.

Of course, I wasn't there, so much of the story is hearsay. The version disseminated by the managers was that Alisha was only a year or so into the role and found the pressure of the job too much, so she left medicine for a less stressful career. The medical staff room version wasn't quite so straightforward, but in the dog-eat-dog world of clinical medicine, this decision was greeted with disdain by the narcissists who gravitated to certain specialties or academia, and one sensed any support evaporated.

By 1994, I had worked at Kilminster as a hematologist for two years. Picture me sitting on a comfortable chair at the back of the consultants dining room, listening to my colleagues and managers working through an agenda that was as effective as any sedative. Probably the worst part of the job was attending mandatory medical staff meetings on a monthly basis. I kept most of the agendas from these get-togethers, and in many I can make out what was written behind my doodles, so am happy to include them in this account of the tragedy that unfolded over the next few years. The agenda rarely changed.

Agenda: Medical Staff Meeting, Monday, June 13, 1994, 5:00 p.m.

Regrets: Daniel Collins.
Minutes of last meeting.
Review of outpatient space.
New junior doctor assessment rubric.
Consultant dining room refurbishment.
Safety of blood products.
Annual leave rules (Miss Dove from HR will present).
Any other business.

At the risk of sounding a little negative about mankind, I already found a quarter of my colleagues utterly intolerable, and occasionally envied Alisha's courage in leaving. The thought of a further thirty years filled me with gloom as I sat through the meeting. Every four weeks Margaret Crocker, our medical director, got all of us together in one room where she chaired a gathering of the Department of Medicine that reminded us how much many of us secretly, or in the case of two of the gastroenterologists openly, despised one another. None of us were fond of going through a rolling agenda of items that, to me, seemed unchanged since at least 1970.

Discussion time for any item was limited to four minutes because Dr. Crocker needed to get back to feed Daphne, her Yorkshire terrier. Whenever it came to making the simplest decisions, we were told by the chair that it would be discussed further at the next meeting. I struggle now to recall any time that an item was discussed and a decision made in one evening.

As Dr. Crocker spoke, I noted a crusty brown inhabitant within her left nostril that seemed to pop out slightly as she exhaled and then retreat again. I was transfixed by the appalling sight and unable to focus on anything on the agenda. I must have glanced away momentarily, because when I looked again, the nostril was empty. Perched on her left bosom, contrasting with the primrose-yellow cashmere sweater, was something resembling a cornflake.

Dr. Crocker was staunchly opposed to private practice. I was neutral; I did none myself but had no ethical issues with it. My main beef with some of the miners of the Golden Nugget seam of private practice was that they were double dipping and not following the spirit of the rules when their non-private practice was reduced to part-time. At about every third medical staff meeting, this subject was raised, but the balance of power in voting lay with the doctors most likely to lose out, so it was never passed.

It seemed to me that to be a medical director one had to metamorphose into a sycophant, creeping around all the hospital managers. Part of the job description appeared to require an urge to see one's name in the *Kilminster Journal*, our local newspaper. If you reached the pinnacle, you might be filmed for local TV showing the site of a new gynecology wing or describing the latest wave of diarrhea to be killing off elderly patients whom God had been calling for the previous six months.

Our chief executive officer, Grace Jones, wasn't invited to our meetings. She was a very pleasant woman given an impossible task. Her role was to help the hospital achieve impossible targets despite a rising population and a shrinking budget. That she couldn't rise to this challenge wasn't entirely her fault. Her real issue was that she despised medical doctors and had spread this philosophy to her management team. Using one of Newton's laws, we could expect an equal and opposite reaction. Indeed, that was exactly the case. This division between clinicians and managers permeated every aspect of our working life.

Thus, medics and management had a challenging relationship. Many of my colleagues blamed the government for the increasing bureaucratization of the health service. We followed the news suggesting the Conservative Party was heading to a major defeat at the next election, and our hope was pinned on a new Labour Party government following through on its commitments to improve health care. Such was our naïveté.

There were plates of Ginger Nuts biscuits at each meeting. Always Ginger Nuts, never another brand throughout my whole career at the hospital. And there were black plastic pots of coffee at the back of the room, with a pump system at the top, often faulty. But at least when things became unbearably tedious, we could legitimately stretch our legs and get coffee. However, there was never any milk, just Coffee-Mate powder. There was something petty about the pleasure some of us felt as we got our coffee and biscuits, interrupting deep conversations about financial cuts and random targets with the snorting of pumps and clatter of plates.

Sitting around the table was bad because we had to engage — it was much better to arrive slightly late and be forced to sit at the back of the room on one of the more comfortable armchairs for an hour's snooze. The meeting always took place in the consultants' dining room, which consisted of a giant table with twenty-two chairs around it and a few armchairs along the wall.

Barbara Leahy, the secretary to the medical director, sat just to the left of Margaret Crocker. She was in her mid-forties and always expensively and immaculately dressed. Barbara had adopted a vicarious power from her current role, and there was always a hint of self-congratulatory "Bet you wish you knew what I know" in the way she set her lips. She knew before any of us who was next in line for a grievance. Barbara also provided the Ginger Nuts.

Clockwise from Barbara sat Richard Headley, a stereotypical cardiologist. I make no apology for this comment, because it was 1994, and in those days, stereotypes were still allowable. He chose to sit near the point of power. I reflected on why anybody would decide to spend thirty years looking after one pump with four valves, in which at least half the patients one saw totally deserved their fates, and in which with few exceptions, one's colleagues were smug and unbearable.

Like all cardiologists, Richard drove some sort of high-end scarlet Audi with a personalized licence plate — in his case, he'd managed to get the letters *EKG* at great expense. He was relatively charming in a superficial, insincere manner, if one liked schmoozers, and apparently handsome if success in getting student nurses and pharma reps to sleep with him was an indication of good looks. Richard was tall and slim with a full head of dark hair and always wore a three-piece suit. He gave the impression that he could have equally had a career as an aftershave or underwear model. Personally, I felt he needed to cut his hair so that it remained above the collar.

My guess would be that he had a private education and was picked for the first XI cricket team and the first XV rugby team to represent his school. My other prediction was divorce for him in the next four years, because eighty percent of cardiologists I'd known, male or female, halved their income at some stage. Hence, my Fourth Rule:

BRIAN'S FOURTH RULE

If you earn more than twice the average income of a doctor, you'll end up divorced and with the average income again. Addendum: If you're dumb enough to get to the Fourth Rule, you're highly likely to fail a second marriage and your ultimate value will be down to twenty-five percent of where you started.

Like all rules, the fourth worked outside medicine, too.

H

At this specific point, I imagine the reader might begin to suspect some long-standing bitterness toward my fellow man. If so, that would be absolutely correct. My wife once accused me of being a misanthrope. When I looked up the word in our dictionary, the definition seemed to fit. I wasn't sure if this was actually a problem, and since it appeared there was nothing I could do about it, other than attempt to pretend to enjoy the company of my fellow man, I accepted her diagnosis.

One might ask if misanthropy was incompatible with being a doctor. I hope this book will clarify that but would add that I never actually chose to be a physician. The role was thrust upon me by my school, which only wished to produce doctors, lawyers, engineers, or financiers. No other careers fitted the independent private school ambitions of the time, other than entering the military — as an officer, of course. You didn't argue with Mr. Pritchett. You obeyed. He was our mathematics teacher. I was petrified of him. A typical interaction between us went as follows.

"Standish, you look confused. There's no such thing as a stupid question. Just ask."

"I'm still not sure what you mean by the word *variable*."

"Standish, I've seen more intelligent amoebae."

I was the only person in the history of my school to go one step farther on the "last-to-be-picked" process. For any team event in which there were "captains" choosing their teams — Richard Headley's kin, no doubt — I was so certain I was regarded as a burden that I grew immune to the sighs and groans from the team ending up with me. I didn't even feel disappointed, since I'd been hardened by this over many years. It wasn't that they disliked me; it was more that they knew my presence on any team drastically increased the odds of failure. I've never been able to kick a soccer ball and only caught a cricket ball about three times in my life, one of which was by accident. Anyone finding my keys didn't toss them to me because they knew I'd spend five minutes trying to get them out from under a table.

One particular week at school, at the age of fourteen, I had an opportunity to redeem myself. In rugby trials, every boy in the school had a chance to be selected for one of four sections: Block One for future cardiologists and financiers who found all sports easy, Blocks Two and Three for the folks in the middle of the pack, and Block Four for kids so utterly useless that a group of amputees could have played better.

That day I knew I'd played like a god and would be Block Two material. I'd caught the ball and run with it, gaining a hundred yards, while my school friends looked on in total confusion that I'd achieved so much. A few seconds later, a bear of a boy who had reached puberty at eight flattened me. But I knew I'd done enough to impress the physical education teacher, who like all PE instructors across the land also taught geography.

The following day, after the trials, the block lists were posted on a noticeboard outside the chapel with great reverence by the school secretary, who always wore a tweed jacket and sensible lace-up shoes. She acted as if this had been a tradition since medieval times. The school had such a sense of greatness — none deserved — that I was surprised there wasn't a fanfare of trumpets as the lists were pinned up. As the secretary walked away, some boys crowded around the lists, then gradually drifted away, chatting excitedly. I waited for them to move off to check where my name was. Oddly, it wasn't in Blocks Two or Three. *Damn it, I'm in Block Four*, I thought. But no, not there, either. A flicker of excitement ran through me when I realized I'd played so well that I was in Block One.

As I stared at my name on the list, the headmaster put his hand on my shoulder. "Brian, you aren't really even up to Block Four, but I had a fantastic idea. You can walk my dog around the playing fields each Tuesday instead of playing rugger."

Other than mild offence at not being good enough, I already felt this could be a winner: (one) I'd get home sooner; (two) I wouldn't have to indulge in the communal baths the rest of the boys seemed to love. There was something utterly ghastly about twenty pubescent boys sharing one giant bathtub twenty feet across. To miss this alone made it worth going on a weekly dog walk. I pictured myself with a handsome black Labrador looking disdainfully at the motley throng standing around cold and bored, hoping not to find themselves holding the ball watching Guy Faulkner charging toward them. Guy was six foot two by the age of twelve and already shaving twice a day.

I hadn't realized at that point that the dog was a Jack Russell terrier with a broken spine after being run over by one of my classmates' mothers, so it walked in a style somewhat akin to a freshly landed salmon. It took ninety minutes to walk around three rugby pitches.

Cricket season saw me still doing the dog walks, mainly because at the trials I'd noticed a lot of daisies growing in the grass at my feet and started making daisy chains when the ball trickled past me without me even seeing it. Let's face it, cricket can be a little dull. I continued to walk Pip, the crippled dog, and daydreamed my way through school until I left.

H

I was daydreaming now at the medical staff meeting. To the left of Headley sat Larry Yen, endocrinologist. A cardboard cutout with his image on it would be indiscernible. He rarely spoke, never smiled, never even nodded or shook his head. Other than one occasion in my whole time at the hospital that I'll get to later, I don't believe his facial expression ever changed.

Then there was the gastroenterologist Colin Marks, a full-time National Health Service employee who somehow managed two or three days per week at the private British United Provident Association hospital, better known as the Golden Nugget. He was in his fifties but looked nearer seventy, owing to a strong relationship with Johnny Walker and cigarillos. His opinion was solid if he could be pinned down to see a non-paying patient. Colin was quite happy to leave his patients to his junior doctors. "Call me any time, but remember, it's a sign of weakness," he'd say, chuckling with nicotine-stained rat's teeth and grinning alarmingly.

I recalled Colin many years earlier when I was a junior doctor. We had twice been called to see a very sad case of a sixteen-year-old boy with anorexia nervosa who had been in the psychiatric ward for six months, gradually declining despite every intervention from the psychiatrist. Dr. Marks had twice been consulted over the boy's abdominal pain and had once again been asked to review some new symptoms. He was dismissive and sent me along with the registrar, who was a year ahead of me and wanted a career in gastroenterology. She examined the boy carefully and pronounced very confidently that he had an abdominal mass and a fistula, and that the diagnosis was clearly not anorexia but probably Crohn's disease.

There were many lessons that day on confirmation bias, the tendency to make everything fit a previously assumed diagnosis, and on the need to perform a physical examination. This young boy hadn't had a physical exam for six months and had languished in a psychiatric ward. Sometimes the lesson wasn't what you would do but what you wouldn't do.

Colin's gastroenterology colleague, Mary Taylor, was seated directly behind him on the extra chairs lined against the wall, the better not to have to catch his eye. They never spoke, either professionally or socially. I was unsure what historical disaster had led to the current impasse. Mary herself was severe and humourless. Her mouth was always a horizontal slit that made her seem furious at all times. Her junior doctors lived in constant anxiety, and the nurses did their best to avoid working or indeed interacting with her at all. She was five foot ten and as skinny as a rake. Her hair was short and the colour people called mousy. Her patients were in the gastroenterology ward on level three. It was a gloomy place, with a staff room that chilled visitors to the bone owing to constant inter-personal tension. There was one male nurse whose role was to navigate the inter-female wars and often act as mediator. According to Richard Headley, who was known to make the occasional inappropriate remark, the ward had the atmosphere one recognizes when the wrong estrogens build up to toxic levels.

Suddenly, I heard someone say, "Brian?"

I glanced up. I hadn't been listening and was somewhere in 1974. It was Jeremiah Foch, one of the managers in the department. At six feet six tall, six feet six in circumference, he wasn't a man to meet in any corridor. He had a long brown beard and a slightly biblical air that matched his name.

To be a hospital manager in Kilminster General required a mind devoid of all inquiry and imagination. The only goal in our hospital was to collect data for whatever target was currently fashionable and to make sure we kept our jobs. Managers traditionally sat to the right of the main table in chairs against the wall where Mary Taylor was currently sitting, each holding a clipboard or folder and writing furiously, as if not scrib-bling duplicate notes was a sign of complacency. Jeremiah had a sidekick whose name I never knew. She was about twenty-five with a forgettable face and large glasses from a decade earlier. It shouldn't have annoyed me, but she kept a cheap ballpoint pen stuck through her bun.

I should mention that I find it hard to maintain focus in any meeting lasting longer than five minutes. The question today was typically inane, something about a recent directive from Public Health regarding the safety of blood products. The managers' aim around blood products was to avoid all public scrutiny lest peeling away the layers of incompetence and dishonesty might expose them to litigation. We were being asked to refrain from publicly commenting on an article that had recently appeared in a national newspaper.

I was being asked if I'd read the directive, which I hadn't, since it had never actually been sent to me. After that, the chair quickly moved on, since any debate could cause her to get home later than planned, and thus the item was carried over to our next gathering. The meeting was adjourned, most issues were carried over for a month, and we all filtered out of the room.

That evening it was late-night shopping in town, and I had to drive down to meet my wife in the market square. Catherine needed a new coat and required my help in choosing it. We ended up in the House of Frazer and had whittled things down to two coats.

"Blue one or red one?" she asked.

I'd been caught in this trap before. "I'd say pretty much equal."

"I think I prefer red."

"Yes, red really suits you."

"Oh, so you hate me in blue?"

I have no recollection which one she bought or whether she ever wore the coat again.

3

Secretaries and Scones

Work on Tuesday was dominated by interpersonal strife between my two secretaries, which had come to a head. My first secretary, Tina Walsh, was excellent when she started. She was appointed the week I joined the hospital and for a while was fun to work with until she met the man who became her husband, a rather controlling aluminum saucepan salesman who stamped out any joy she'd ever shown. Tina had begun her breeding program, and upon arrival of the first child, Sinbad — yes, indeed, Sinbad — she'd elected, quite reasonably, to come back part-time by which stage she was already heavy with her second child. That meant I had to find a new part-time person to fill the gap.

I ended up with the experienced secretary of a retired colleague. Dorothy Pollard was a woman who soon developed the delusion that she was my mother and who was very protective. She could type the letters from twenty clinic patients, sort out all the resulting administration, sneak out to smoke two cigarettes, and chat incessantly to anybody passing the office door, yet was still more efficient than any other secretary in the hospital.

The inevitable challenge was that Tina felt hugely threatened by a usurper in her space — unnecessarily in my opinion — and started decorating her desk and monitor with pictures of her rather ugly baby and her beagle, which weighed at least two hundred pounds.

Dorothy innocently put these distractions in the desk drawer every Wednesday and Friday when she worked. As soon as Tina was back in, she returned the pictures to their places, usually with muttered complaints. Before I knew it, battle lines were drawn. Had the baby and the dog not been quite so hideous, I would have had more sympathy, but I could see why Dorothy found both creatures devoid of charm. Combat ensued for several weeks, escalating at an alarming rate, with increasingly devious plots to discredit the other secretary: messages not passed on, results not attached to notes and left for the other to do. The final straw was when the photo of the fat beagle disappeared completely and a moustache was drawn on the baby. With a twinkle in her eye, Dorothy denied doing any of this. For my part, I had enough to think about without their conflicts.

Now I heard footsteps along the corridor and the sound of car keys being rubbed along one of the cast-iron radiators in the corridor. I was in the old part of the hospital in the original building: high ceilings, damp walls, dim lights, and at my end of the corridor, the ever-present, vague smell of dead rat.

Richard Headley strolled into my office, tossing his Audi keys in his hand. "Got two minutes, Brian?"

"Sure, but can I go first? I need you to help solve my secretarial warfare."

"Okay, tell me about it."

I quickly explained how my attempts at rationalizing the inter-secretarial strife had failed.

Headley nodded, then said, "Why don't I take on Tina full-time and you just have Dorothy?"

At that stage, I'd only seen laudable motives from Richard, but since he was apparently hormonally driven in almost every decision, I feared that poor Tina might eventually feel harassed. Having thought that, it became clear to me that coming to work was an escape from her husband for Tina, so when I asked her in the presence of Richard about the new arrangement, she seemed excited to work full-time for Headley. His charm was impressive. I did promise her later that if anything untoward occurred, she could come back to hematology. In any event, she immediately started packing her belongings and seemed prepared to waltz down the corridor to scope out her new office with a new light in her eyes. Within ten minutes or so it, appeared Headley had found a solution that pleased everybody. He gave Tina a large white grin, winked at her, and invited her to join him for lunch in town the following day to discuss her new role. She blushed and nodded shamelessly.

Once the deal was done, Headley gave me some blood-work results. "Brian, can you interpret this for me?"

Outside the four chambers of the heart, Richard's medical knowledge was just slightly lower than the *Reader's Digest Family Health Guide*. His query about blood work felt like a pretext for something more pressing.

I sensed he needed to share another matter, since he didn't give any indication that he wanted to go. "Richard, I have to get back to the children before bedtime."

"No problem. I'll walk with you."

I had that strange British class discomfort that I fear would stay with me for life. We were completely different in almost every way. Richard came from a privileged background, son of Sir Stanley Headley, whose financial and media empire was legendary. I was always a little intimidated by these individuals, though we oddly seemed to get on better than the system would predict.

Part of the issue was that I'd been surrounded by these individuals for years at school where I clearly didn't belong. I was one of only four boys at my private boys' school who had won a scholarship for a "free place." This should have been a great honour and opportunity, but to this day I wonder how much private single-sex education damages human beings. Was that where my misanthropy seed was planted?

Most of the other boys were middle class and paid fees. My family was never poor but never rich, though to hear my mother talk, we were royalty. Without the scholarship, I never would have gone to that school.

My family had one car, a chocolate-brown twenty-year-old Rover that my mother felt raised our social status, and that my dad paid me ten pence to wash each weekend until I used a Brillo pad to remove some bird poo, after which I was fired from that role. The honour was given to my brother, Harvey. Every other boy at the school was driven in a Mercedes or a BMW. Meanwhile, I preferred to take the bus, but when I was driven, I urged my father to drop me off a couple of streets away to avoid the smirks of the other boys when our Rover rattled into the school spewing black smoke from the exhaust. The boys at the school were already convinced of their superior place in British society.

To earn money, I did a milk round before school. However, the milk round days were coming to a close. Mostly, the bottles were washed out. But there were always households with bottles covered in sour milk that got on my trousers, so I'd have to rush home and change before catching the bus to school. We were in the middle of a few days of power cuts during which we ate supper under candlelight and the washing piled up, so there was always the risk I'd go to school smelling of sour milk. I decided time was up for that job.

In any case, the milk round was traumatic for other reasons. Mr.

Stickley, the headmaster of a different school and one of the people to whom I delivered milk, shouted at me because blue tits pecked the foil at the top of his bottle, and "surely," he told me, "you aren't so intellectually bereft that you don't recognize the purpose of these plastic cups?" It turned out I was indeed intellectually bereft, because it never occurred to me that the three plastic cups were left outside the door for that reason. I was also a coward and was petrified even passing the house thereafter, though I found it fun to imagine the various bad ends that might befall Mr. Stickley. He was the only one on the whole milk round who insisted on having skim milk. My granddad told me they used to save that for pigs when he was younger, which gave me some comfort.

I needed a different way to earn pocket money.

School was on the other side of town from our home. I had ten pence per day each way for the bus, but I only caught it in the morning, while in the evening I walked all the way home so that by each Saturday I had fifty pence. Some of this I spent on a half ounce of rhubarb-and-custard sweets. The rest I saved.

I thought about all of this as Headley and I entered the lift together. When the doors began to close, I spotted Oliver Michaels breaking into a mincing run to catch it.

"Hold the lift!" he shouted in his strong Welsh accent.

I made an impressive show of bashing the lift wall next to the open-door button and smiled to myself as the doors closed despite my apparent sterling attempt to help him. That day I failed. Just as the doors came together a hand appeared between them, and the doors opened once more, allowing Michaels in, condemning us to hold our breath as his halitosis reached every corner of the lift.

It was one thing to be stuck in a lift with a conceited upper-class serial philanderer, but Michaels produced an extreme instant antibody reaction. There wasn't just one specific thing. More accurately, a whole collection of irritations made him unbearable. The gestalt package included a Welsh accent, which God created to be like hearing a beautiful melodic poem but from Oliver grated on every nerve. His teeth, always in a smile, were like big yellow Scrabble tiles. His skin had a constant greasy glow as if he'd smeared Vaseline all over his face, while his hair was a tight curl. Even his walk annoyed me. Despite being six foot two, he took strides of about twelve inches so that he always gave the illusion of being in an enormous hurry. And as already mentioned, he could be sniffed from at least ten feet away, the sort of stench encountered when a bucket of leaves sitting behind a shed for a year or so was finally emptied out.

I wonder if I had an unconscious bias against the Welsh.

My mother insisted we were better than many people and had a list of random groups of humans who were beneath us and also sometimes beneath contempt, including, but not limited to the Welsh, the Irish, the Scots, the French, anybody with a strong regional accent other than her own, and anyone who was "common," never clearly defined.

She had strong opinions on all issues and banned us from watching ITV — for common people — though I noted she enjoyed *The Benny Hill Show* and *The Six Million Dollar Man*.

Unexpectedly, she was an ardent fan of gay people because my Uncle Paul who lived up the road was openly gay and told us riotous stories of trips to Sydney, Australia, once a year. On the other hand, his own father was persona non grata in the house because he'd tried to kiss my mum in the kitchen when my dad was in the next room. Dad never said anything to him, but I think all involved parties understood the situation. These were all things that at the time seemed totally normal in our lives.

Now Michaels asked me if I was happy with the new office space arrangements. I thought he was referring to the secretaries and agreed wholeheartedly.

"Well, that's wonderful. I'll let Jeremiah know it's a done deal. I think you'll be very happy in the basement." While Michaels said this, he immersed me in a cloud of foul fumes before exiting the lift.

Headley never got his chance to discuss what was on his mind.

In my pocket when I got home were three or four memos. Emails hadn't become the scourge of humans yet. I started reading: "With the expansion of the endoscopy suite and the recruitment of new consultants, office space will be at a premium. The medical director has decided that the hematologists will share a desk and be relocated to Fleming Wing." There was no invitation to discuss this. It was a fait accompli. I'd been hijacked by the managers and gastroenterology who had been on a land-grabbing mission for years. And in my innocence, I'd agreed to the whole deal in the lift. *Plus ça change.* Rather gallingly, I gathered Jeremiah Foch had agreed to release some funds to renovate the dank old office wing before the new group moved in.

I arrived home to find Catherine had been baking. There were sixteen cheese scones on a rack in the kitchen. They were still warm and perfectly golden, so I reached for one.

"No, you can't touch," Catherine told me. "There's a broken one there you can taste."

"Amazing. These are perfect. Best ever."

"What was wrong with the last ones?"

The perfect sixteen scones were transferred to a tin container labelled "Quality Street." We forgot them, of course, and they were thrown away stale two weeks later.

4

A Pretty Bad Month

Agenda: Medical Staff Meeting, Monday, December 4, 1995

Regrets: Daniel Collins.
Minutes of last meeting.
Review of outpatient space.
New junior doctor assessment rubric.
Consultant dining room future use proposal.
Discussion on physician communication with media.
Annual leave rules (Miss Dove from HR will present the amended form).
Any other business.

The meeting was as dull as ever, and I couldn't concentrate because I was in the doghouse. We had a rule at home that once a toilet was cleaned that for reasons lost in the mists of time nobody used it for a few hours so that for a while we could bask in the porcelain white glow of total purity. I'd failed. It had been four minutes. I rather foolishly attempted to rationalize this decision to use the toilet rather than walk upstairs and perform exactly the same process, but Catherine was disdainful of my pathetic attempts. I understood now that it wasn't for me to understand these arrangements, only to obey.

To make matters worse, I'd apparently left a tissue in the pocket of my trousers before they went in to the washing machine. On the scale of sins that I repeated on a monthly basis, this was near the top, though I always felt the level of dissatisfaction it produced to be a little out of proportion to the crime.

The only saving grace for an otherwise tedious month was the Christmas party the previous weekend. In general, I avoided all group events, but Catherine insisted we attend for at least an hour to avoid getting a reputation, because I'd so far avoided every one of these occasions since my appointment. It was pretty much as I expected: everybody unnaturally happy, and whenever talking to me, casting their gazes around for somebody more interesting to speak to.

I could have predicted the menu before I got there. The starter was a limp salad, the main course chicken supreme on a stone-cold plate. Dessert was a meringue nest with fruit salad from a can. To make matters worse, tradition had it that the consultants bought the alcohol, and I somehow found myself with about fifteen members of the pathology department ordering drinks on my tab. I knew the names of three of them.

Catherine insisted on dancing and enjoying herself while I found a quiet corner to sit and appear content in my own company. I spotted Headley dancing in an overly erotic fashion with a junior nurse from his ward. His wife had stayed at home, I gathered. The low point of the evening was when the gossip started that one of the urologists had carnal knowledge with my own junior doctor in the Kilminster Manor swimming pool halfway through the evening. He was a three-times divorced man and permanently in heat. My only personal concern was the swimming pool water, and from that day on, I vowed never to take a dip in that soup of bodily fluids. There was no way I'd trust a filter when it came to a colleague's secretions.

The evening ground on. The next time I saw Headley he was slow-dancing with someone to an Annie Lennox song. I looked again, and to my horror, realized it was Tina Walsh, my previous secretary. She had her hands intertwined behind his neck, and there seemed to be less air between them than most would consider decent. He took her to the bar to get her a whisky. "One finger or two?" he asked with a meaningful twinkle in his eye.

Thankfully, we used our babysitter excuse, which usually presented the perfect justification for an early departure.

"I thought you said your mother was staying at your house to look after the children," accused the pathology department secretary, two flecks of meringue stuck to her chin. I ignored her but made a mental note that she was trouble.

On Tuesday, Krishna Ramachandran, internal medicine, asked me to review a young patient with probable leukemia. Krishna was an ever-smiling genius reputed to have been passed over four times for chair of medicine at the local medical school despite twice the number of peer-reviewed publications to the closest competitor. In typical medical doctor fashion, everyone was appalled and nobody said a thing. Their loss was our gain, and once more the community hospitals of the National Health Service were propped up by the best of India. Krishna had spent his whole career at Kilminster, along the way chairing four national committees, and had several publications in academic journals each year. He was also a favourite of medical students, especially around exam time, because he always stayed behind after work two evenings a week to take them to see interesting patients.

Krishna was in his late fifties. He was a very thin Indian who despite an athletic appearance had severe coronary artery disease. One of his daughters used to babysit our kids, so we knew his family well. In fact, she booked the coming Friday so that Catherine and I could see the new James Bond movie *Goldeneye*. Having told me about the case, Dr. Ramachandran scurried off to a meeting, and I found my way up to the medical wards.

Searching for his patient's chart in the notes trolley, I found it and pulled it out. Richard Headley was nearby and noticed who I was about to see. With a grin, he said, "She's got a toast factor of nine out of ten, mate. Have you ever had a patient who didn't die?"

I ignored him and his vile sense of humour. The patient was on her own in a side room. Her name was Amanda. "And do people call you Mandy?" I asked.

"Amanda, not Mandy."

Bad start, I thought.

Amanda was seventeen, was as pale as the pillow she was lying on, and had a large cold sore on her lower lip. Attempting a smile, she tried to sit up a little in the bed. Amanda had been on the ward for two weeks already, having initially been admitted with severe pneumonia. Her bedside table was covered with get-well-soon cards, two vases of flowers, and a picture of a small girl that I took to be her younger sister cuddled up to an old black Labrador with a grey muzzle. There was also a photograph of Amanda riding a large black horse.

I took a chair, sat beside her bed, and we began to chat, not concerning her symptoms but about her horse, which nobody else knew how to ride the way she did. She told me her mother had died a few years ago of a drug overdose. Her sister had passed away age five in this hospital. She lived at home with her father, who was an English teacher in the local independent school. Amanda was doing well at school despite the poor hand of cards life had dealt her and had already been accepted by the University of Cambridge to read history.

"Do you know why you're here?" I asked.

"Dr. Krishna told me he thought I had leukemia." She said that calmly but with a look of apprehension. Her next words were tough to hear. "I'm going to die, aren't I? That will leave Dad with nobody." It was rare to have a young patient be so direct.

At the time, I was still learning how to communicate — I believed it took about thirty years to become reasonably competent at which point one retired. I was always honest and agreed with Amanda that we were in a sticky situation and that without treatment things would only get worse. However, I told her the current treatments had produced some amazing remissions.

I always tried to leave the door for hope open at least a crack. "This is even potentially curable. It isn't going to be easy, and it's not going to be fast, but we're going to fight this together." I didn't tell her the odds or let her know all the facts. At this point, she needed to hear this, I felt.

"When do we start?" she asked.

"Today."

We spent another fifteen minutes or so talking about what was going to happen, starting with a bone marrow biopsy that I could get done later that day. I had a child not many years younger than her and couldn't even bear to imagine how I'd feel if she became seriously ill.

After that, I went to the office to complete my notes Sitting there, I glanced out the window at the car park and thought back several years to this same hospital when I was a medical student on call for pediatrics one January night.

It was about nine in the evening. A five-year-old girl named Rebecca had been brought in by her aunty who was looking after her and her sister for the weekend while the parents went away for a long weekend to celebrate their tenth wedding anniversary. The aunty had to bring both girls into the hospital, since her husband, who was Rebecca's mother's brother, was still at work in a local tire factory. Very reluctantly, she returned home when the nurses promised to call her regularly about Rebecca's progress, confident that in an hour or two the girl would be over the worst.

"Some steroids, a couple of nebulizers, and some antibiotics will sort this," the nurse said. "She'll probably be able to go home in the morning."

This was a time of Nightingale wards — vast rooms with twelve beds on each side each with a set of curtains that could pull around. Rebecca's ward was empty except for one bed, five up on the left. I never knew why this was the bed where she was placed rather than the closest one to the nurses' desk. Every other bed was vacant. The main lights were off. A yellow wall light glowed above the bed.

A middle grade junior doctor was on call for pediatrics. She'd started four days earlier and had a book in her pocket she constantly referred to for guidance. The junior doctor followed the required protocol, prescribing a mask known as a nebulizer, which noisily provided drugs directly to the lungs to open up the airways. The little girl was given steroids and antibiotics.

Rebecca propped herself up with her arms, desperately trying to get a breath. She kept pulling the mask off, and the nurse firmly and rather harshly ordered her to put it back on. A second and then a third nebulizer were tried. Rebecca looked exhausted and was bluer, but the registrar was satisfied, since she could no longer hear a wheeze. "Beware the silent chest," I recalled from our lectures. That meant not that the asthma was better but that such a small amount of air was moving that it made no noise — a bad prognostic sign.

I was sent off to see another admission with a vomiting illness. As I left, I glanced up the ward at Rebecca, alone with a mask on, the tallow light above her. The registrar was in the office writing up the notes. The nurse, oddly I felt, was sitting at the desk knitting.

And that was the last time I saw Rebecca. She died that evening, alone, frightened, with nobody holding her hand. The consultant hadn't even been phoned or come in that night to check on any of the patients. There was no debrief, no discussion of what could have been done differently.

I finished my on call at eight the following morning, a heavy weight on my soul. There was a dense, wet mist in the air as I walked to the car park and got into my car. Turning on the radio, I heard Carly Simon singing "Coming Around Again." Somehow the song gained a new meaning and poignancy for me. I probably sat there for an hour. Something had changed. Medicine had lost its glamour already.

That was the first young patient I saw die. I didn't blame the doctor at all and never really knew if the outcome could have been different. By then, I'd seen a range of procedural errors in unsupervised junior doctors, the only linking theme being they were never discussed. I was in the wrong profession and knew it. But I felt I was trapped on a single road that would lead me on a journey I wasn't ready to take for the rest of my career.

Rarely a day had gone by since that evening when the image of the dying child, and the imagination of her parents' grief and guilt didn't return to my thoughts. I was already wrestling with my own interpretation of the events leading up to the prescription of infected factor VIII to patients with hemophilia, which had resulted in many of them becoming afflicted with hepatitis C and HIV. I perceived the same themes of cultural institutional silence.

I finished organizing the further tests and initial therapy for Amanda-not-Mandy and prayed to a god who might or might not exist that this time the outcome would be better.

On Wednesday, I always took a sandwich to work in a My Little Pony box Louisa, my nine-year-old daughter, deemed too babyish for school. I couldn't bear to see it go to waste, preferring to spend my money on strangers at Christmas staff parties, though I sympathized with my daughter's position. Now I opened it, and inside was a chutney sandwich I'd made for old time's sake.

When I was twelve, my dad rented a garage to a dodgy man with a sheepskin jacket who was in the cleaning supply business. After three months, he'd paid no rent and had disappeared, leaving four large boxes of toilet paper made from some sort of non-absorbent parchment paper, along with twelve four-litre bottles of industrial floor cleaner, which actually was so ammoniacal that it smelled like urine. In addition, there was a box containing five hundred white paper bags with an image of a woman in a polka-dot dress and the words "Feminine hygiene products, please dispose in bin provided" in small letters underneath.

My mother had made some green tomato chutney. In fact, she'd prepared thirty jars owing to a bumper tomato crop that summer. It wasn't particularly good — a little runny and bitter. But I had, of course, told her it was delicious. Every single day of school until I left home three years later, I had a sandwich with green tomato chutney and cheddar cheese in a small white paper bag with a polka-dot woman on the front.

Thankfully, my father deemed the toilet paper to be unsatisfactory and gave it to my grandad, who was delighted and felt this was a step forward from his own arrangements.

Amanda had completed her first chemotherapy treatment, and over the next few days her risk of infection rose, so she had to be nursed under a very strict regimen of sterility. We had three such isolation rooms, and I currently had a patient in each, two with leukemia, and one with septicemia related to AIDS. The stigma related to his diagnosis was ridiculous, and I'd even noticed that staff went out of their way to avoid entering his room.

On Saturday, our youngest daughter, Martha, who was eight, was invited to a birthday party. To avoid the parents of the birthday girl having to supervise other people's children at the event, the parents of the invited friends were asked to come, too. It took place at a local farm where an adventure playground was set up in a converted barn with a few rope nets and a ball pool. Anyone walking in there was greeted with the unmistakable smell of sweaty children, noxious bodily gases and secretions, and a discernible background odour of sheep dung.

While I stated earlier that I found twenty-five percent of my colleagues annoying, I could unequivocally state that I couldn't stand ninety-five percent of OPK or other people's kids. I sat there with the parents of two highly intelligent children telling me how their private tutor gave calculus lessons when Cordelia was four, and how at home they always spoke Mandarin, since she was headed for a career in the diplomatic service. I could barely think of one couple whose kids didn't repulse me.

Children who run up to my table when I go for a meal, their parents beaming at me as if I, too, love the fluorescent-yellow-snotted, smelly, feral urchin staring at me, was something I couldn't bear. In fact, I was thinking of writing a handbook on how to avoid children irritating other adults who didn't have children with them. However, a wise friend once advised me: "Never comment on other people's parenting skills." All my life I struggled to follow that particular recommendation. Personally, I thought such a book could be a bestseller and save many friendships. There are a few simple rules, including:

- If you invite me and Catherine for dinner, put your child to bed.

- If you talk to me and your child comes along and interrupts, don't stop speaking to me and indulge the rude little brat.
- Don't make your kid sing a song to me as a performance.
- If you go out for a meal, keep your children at your own table.
- If you fly, write to me first so I can book a different plane.
- At all times wipe their noses.
- When you change a nappy while visiting me, don't put the dirty one in my bin.
- Don't tell me your children are exceptionally gifted. They aren't. They're highly likely to be average.
- Don't arrange extra Greek lessons for your child in the evening, since that's a sure guarantee that by twenty-two, he or she will be taking recreational drugs.
- Don't tell me that Rupert got the prize for maths. I don't care.
- I also don't care when your child was potty-trained. Potty-training at twelve months doesn't predict a future prime minister.
- I especially don't care if your children have somehow communicated to you that they're vegan. If they come to my house, they'll get dinosaur-shaped chicken nuggets.

My own children, needless to say, were actually quite adorable and well behaved, and I believed our parenting skills were second to none.

5

Suffering Christmas

Every week over the next year was like the previous ones, and before I knew it, in December 1996, I received an invitation to the next Kilminster General Christmas party. Once again, it was to take place at Kilminster Manor. The menu was circulated: a salad starter, chicken supreme or a vegetarian lasagne, followed by meringue nests.

All I can remember about that year's party, other than the food, was that we ended up sitting at a table with Trevor Nichol, an orthopedic surgeon who was there with his wife, Peggy. She worked in a sperm donation clinic and consequently was always invited to parties, since there seemed to be a thousand stories and a universal fascination with the process. Most parties ended up in the kitchen with Peggy in full flow, usually about having to sterilize the ejaculation cubicle at the end of each day and which cleaning agents were best.

Presumably owing to the professional rules of whatever the sperm collection agency association was called, she was somewhat vague about how the female participant chose her product, but she explained that there were characteristics one could request such as height, eye colour, and ethnicity. Undoubtedly, nobody ever chose a bald, fat guy with an IQ of seventy.

Interestingly, out of the previous hundred samples deposited, all they had left were the sperm of twenty gingers that were flushed down the toilet on the last day of the month. The clinic manager pushed her to persuade women to select the ginger sperm rather than waste it, and she was able to use sixteen. After that, I looked out for ginger-haired kids and always wondered. But hard though it was to imagine, there were worse scenarios than buying ginger sperm. As I glanced over at Nigel Robinson, a colleague whose DNA must never be passed on, I had an unpleasant, almost realistic hallucination of him actively donating to the clinic and regurgitated some baked brie as I considered what safeguards existed to block the transmission of his genetic material to mankind.

What was routine to a hematologist was the nadir in the life of most patients. The treatments got better every year, and I believed I was becoming better at talking to patients. However, I was never able to embrace the culture of medicine, and in my heart, I wanted to be as far away from the role as possible. Perhaps an engineer? Maybe learn to lay hedges? Perhaps build drystone walls or clean the floor at the sperm donor clinic?

Some of my school friends had become stockbrokers and had already retired. I wasn't sure that would appeal, either. But almost anything else other than my current career would be an improvement.

Amanda was in a four-month remission, and we had an excellent relationship. I was beginning to record a few more successful remissions — we never called them cures — but there were too many patients we'd lost and every one weighed heavily on my soul. I'd lost four hemophilia patients in the previous year to AIDS-related infections. It was clear with those patients they'd been given the factor VIII protein in blood infected with HIV and hepatitis C long after it was known the risk existed. Not one of these patients had even been told either that the risk existed or indeed that they'd been tested for the virus. I watched young men have their lives stolen and families torn apart by an illness, in my opinion, acquired as a result of multiple layers of incompetence, deceit, and some-times arrogance.

One of my patients bought me some Christmas socks. They had little buttons that when pressed played music for twenty seconds or so. Another patient baked a cake that Catherine refused to eat, claiming she saw a grey pubic hair sticking out of the top.

We had an enormous stroke of luck when Catherine developed flu the day before the Pathology Department Christmas get-together. Of course, I was hugely apologetic to everybody that we'd be unable to attend. I even popped into town and bought a large tin of Quality Street for the pathology department. I wasn't certain, but I think one of the lab techni-cians muttered, "Last of the big spenders," as I departed.

On Christmas Eve, another young patient of forty-two died of leukemia. It was my job to share this expected but still devastating news. Why was it always worse to die at Christmas?

I squatted in front of the man's wife in the relatives' room and was about to open my mouth when I heard "Rudolph the Red-Nosed Reindeer" playing somewhere. The music confused me, and I stopped talking for a moment.

When I realized my Christmas socks were the culprit, I was mortified and surreptitiously reached down to press the button to turn them off. Instead, the music just moved forward to "Jingle Bells," whereupon I clenched the sock and ankle, hoping to dampen the sound of the jolly festive songs. The patient's wife said nothing. Even now, twenty years later, I wonder if I got away with it. Suffice it to say, I never wore musical socks again.

Christmas Day was spent at my mother's. She always enjoyed having us over for a couple of days. My brother, Harvey, was there, too, uncharacteristically a little more morose than usual.

On New Year's Eve, I was called into work. A newly referred patient needed to be seen in the Emergency Department. Depressingly, it was yet another one with a new diagnosis of leukemia, a young mother of two. We ended up admitting her to the ward, promising to return the next morning, grimly wondering if this would be the last new year for the thirty-two-year-old.

It was midnight. As I headed back toward the car park, there was the barely conscious body of a young university student who had been brought in drunk and who had tried to take his own discharge. He had lain in front of the hospital entrance and vomited. His last thought before slipping into an alcoholic sleep was to write "Happy New Year" in his own vomit.

I hoped it would be.

6

Who Knew My Brother Was Gay?

When I arrived home that New Year's Day 1997, the answering machine was flashing. There was a message from my brother telling me he was HIV positive. Of course, it was somewhat more complex than that. The message was garbled and barely audible, obviously made from a public phone booth where there were clearly several drunken revellers passing by. In the message, he threatened he was going to climb to the end of a tower crane next to St. Mary's Church and jump off. In those times, anybody with a mind to do so could access a crane in a building site, health and safety being applied with less attention to detail than more recently.

At first I thought he was joking, but by the end of his message, I fully understood this was real and ran out of the house to my car, not even wishing Catherine a happy new year. I saw her pull the curtain aside and raise her hand to wave, clearly a little puzzled that I was returning to work again having just walked into the house.

And thus I found myself driving to a building site close to the town centre in a fine drizzle of rain at one o'clock in the morning, then sitting there, hoping desperately Harvey wouldn't jump, saying aloud, "Don't be such a plonker. We're planning a New Year's Day country walk and pub lunch tomorrow. If you're going to kill yourself, at least time it better."

I raised my head to see the crane, which was vaguely lit by yellow lights from the road, along with a single strong white flood from the cabin on the tower. When I couldn't make out any figure either on the arm of the crane or climbing down, I began to question whether my brother was even there. Suddenly, the passenger door opened, and Harvey collapsed into the seat, saying nothing.

"I guess you need to tell me what's up. It's not going to be as bad as you think, whatever it is, Harv. And if it's money again, we can fix it."

"I've got HIV."

It's actually quite tough to know how to respond to what Harvey had just told me until faced with it. In the mid-1990s, there was still a huge stigma associated with a diagnosis of HIV, even a sense, for some, that it was a death sentence.

While I was searching for words that weren't platitudes, Harvey asked, "Did you know I was gay?"

That should have been a perfect comedy moment. Instead, I merely stared at him and grinned. "When Dad said you'd be going to the local boys' school if you didn't start working harder, you looked as if it was Christmas. You go on holidays to Sydney every year with Uncle Paul at the same time as the city's Gay and Lesbian Mardi Gras. You spent twelve months living with Simon Milford who's the gayest florist in town. And you just asked me if I knew you were gay."

"Oh, my God! Do you think anybody else knows? What about Mum?"

"She knows and said out of the one hundred interesting things about you, it ranked at ninety-nine."

He smiled ruefully. "What was one hundred?"

I noticed his hands were shaking. "I guess the truth is, I'm not entirely surprised by what you just told me, but I'm still shocked, if that's not a contradiction."

We sat in the car for two hours and talked. I assumed Catherine thought I was working and knew I might be in the hospital for half the night, so I wasn't worried about her.

Harvey told me that despite knowing the risks, he'd spent much of the late 1980s taking no precautions whatsoever. "My friends told me that catching HIV was inevitable and it was best to get it over with."

He said that by the time he did know more about it he'd already decided he was invincible and destined to escape it. "I saw a doctor today who confirmed the diagnosis. He seemed pretty judgmental to be honest."

Harvey felt the advice he was given seemed to be based on ignorance and prejudice. "The doctor more or less told me there's nothing that'll alter my fate. I just have to carry on and wait for things to progress. His last words were 'Go home and wait.' Can you believe that?"

We talked further and agreed there were now potentially effective treatment options.

"But I love swimming," Harvey said. "I can't do that anymore. And I can't really go shopping. And does it matter if I don't like Elton John?" He agreed to come to my house rather than his own place alone.

"You'll have to sleep on a blow-up mattress in the back room," I said. "As you know, we don't have a spare bedroom."

Tomorrow everything would be closed for New Year's Day, and Harvey had already taken time off until the following Monday, so we had a little time to deal with his situation.

"One thing, Brian, promise me you won't tell Mum."

I nodded. "But I'll have to share with Catherine."

When we got to my house, I threw a couple of sheets and a blanket to him as he sat on the floor blowing up the mattress. "Just tell me this, though, Harv. Why couldn't you just have one partner? Why did you have to make this a mission to have sex with as many men as possible?"

"Because if a gay couple say they're happily married and only have eyes for each other, they're lying. Gay men are sluts, Brian. I'm just a slutty dog." He actually smiled his best full smile. "At least Dad never knew."

"That you have HIV or that you're gay?"

"Both. I was always his favourite."

Our dad had died several years earlier. He was a man of unwavering opinions who seemed able to live his life around a limited number of statements and a theme of pessimism such as "never trust a man with a beard" and "every third person is a thief." He also said: "I'll be lucky to live to forty," followed, after he reached forty, with "I'll be lucky to reach fifty." Ironically, he actually reached both fifty and sixty but didn't make it to sixty-one.

Dad passed away on Boxing Day. We had finished lunch and the family was in the living room playing charades. We all wanted to watch the movie *The Great Escape*, which Dad had apparently seen thirty-two times, but custom on Boxing Day dictated we keep the television off and instead play games whether desired or not. When it was Dad's turn, he indicated his choice was a film, three words, first word *The*.

"*Alice in Wonderland!*" shouted Granny.

"First word is *The*, Mum," said our mother.

"*Crocodile Dundee?*" replied Granny.

Dad put up his hand to signify the second word, then made a motion as if holding a piece of cheese in the right hand and grating it before dramatically falling to the floor.

"*Legends of the Fall!*" cried Harvey.

"Three words!" yelled Mum.

"*The Man Who Fell to Earth!*" shouted cousin Robbie, always a little slow.

"Three words!" Mum lashed out. "Are you actually that stupid?" Slightly cruel, of course, because Robbie was.

Dad then lay on the floor pretending to sleep.

"*The Big Sleep?*" I ventured.

But then there was a ring at the door and the dogs rushed off barking, followed by the rest of us. Aunty Jean had arrived and was always the one to get a party really going.

To this day, I always ask myself two questions: "What was Dad's film title?" and "If we'd actually tried to resuscitate him, would he still be with us?"

Now, with Harvey's mattress inflated, he was unrolling a sleeping bag. It was 4:30 a.m. I had to be up in two hours to walk the dogs.

7

Sally White Shows Her True Colours

At the first medical staff meeting in the new year, it was the same agenda, same sandwiches, same colleagues except for Krishna, who had finally retired a week before Christmas and died three weeks later. That meant he suffered a final indignity: the last face he saw was that of Oliver Michaels. We calculated that it would take two consultants to replace Krishna, both to be chosen by a small group chaired by Richard Headley, which didn't bode well.

Agenda: Medical Staff Meeting, Monday, January 13, 1997

Regrets: Daniel Collins.
Minutes of last meeting.
Review of outpatient space.
New Junior doctor assessment rubric.
Consultant dining room plans for closure.
Hematology issues and communication with media.
Annual leave rules (Miss Dove from HR will present the new revised
    application process).
Any other business.

Speaking of Oliver Michaels, he droned on about outpatient space at the meeting. If something could be said in five words, Oliver made it fifty. He'd lost his audience a long time ago, so Margaret Crocker deferred the subject to the next meeting.

Jeremiah Foch, the middle manager, had the ginger nuts. He took three, then passed the plate with the final biscuit to Crocker, who sighed theatrically and shoved it to the person seated to her left with a characteristic impatient shake of her head. Next to Oliver, Margaret did most of the talking at our staff meetings, mainly employing the words "We'll put this on next month's agenda."

Dr. Crocker had an imperious manner in the overbearing, arrogant meaning of the word. She always had a silk scarf or shawl draped around her, and her spectacles were worn at the very tip of her nose, allowing her to scrutinize people over the top of them. I was sure a good optometrist could have given her bifocals, but I figured she enjoyed the image. Her hair was flicked up at the front and probably cost a fortune but increased her resemblance to Christopher Walken.

Sally White, another cardiologist, had started a month before Krishna died and was the opposite of him in almost every way. She had an item in "any other business" and was making a bid for more outpatient space, mainly, it turned out, to allow her to drop her Friday clinic. Sally was feeling tetchy. I wasn't clear if this was her normal baseline state but suspected she'd been rejected for the third year running in her application to join the annual Canadian seal-clubbing festival in Newfoundland.

Now she looked directly at me. "Brian, I think your Tuesday morning hemophilia clinic may no longer be needed. Can I formally put in a bid for your two clinic rooms?"

I felt the red mist rising and pushed it down.

Sally had moved to the area recently and had bought a small farm. Her husband, Neville Botham, a skinny, slightly effeminate man with body odour, a geography degree, a wispy, unkempt beard, and thick glasses, had decided to become a farmer. I suspected the farmer idea was Sally's, since she ruled over Neville with an iron fist. With the current trends for emu meat and alpaca wool, she'd seen the potential for an independent lucrative business and thus dived headlong into being an emu meat supplier.

Neville ordered twelve eggs from a friend of a university housemate, apparently an emu dealer in Wigan, and bought an incubator from a farm shop in Worcester. Within three days, he had a chilled container containing twelve eggs, nine green and three blue. He transferred the eggs to his incubator, and to his delight fifty-six days later, five hatched, though only three grew into emus. One died at two weeks, the other turned out to be a cassowary. Undeterred, he persisted, albeit investing more in fencing than anticipated, while fielding several complaints from users of the public footpath crossing their land.

"What do you mean?" I finally asked Sally.

"Well, half your patients seem to be dead or dying. It looks like you won't actually need a hemophilia clinic much longer."

I couldn't grace this comment with a response, not trusting my voice. Instead, I rose from my seat and began to leave the room.

Crocker stopped me. "Brian, you can't leave. We need you for item five."

I glanced at the heavily defaced agenda in my hands.

"Yes!" piped up Jeremiah. "I've invited the trust lawyers here today to discuss our current risk exposure related to hematology deaths."

I contemplated his long, vile beard with its flecks of ginger nut and glistening beads of sweat. "You all disgust me," I muttered. "And no, I won't discuss this here."

I once had sixty patients with hemophilia, and now three had died of AIDS and another ten were infected with HIV. Of the remainder, ten had non-A, non-B hepatitis, which had been renamed hepatitis C. That would go down in history as one of the greatest scandals ever in the Health Service, but at present the defences were up at all levels and a formal inquiry had been avoided.

As I left the room, I noticed a thin smile on Sally's lips and a raised right eyebrow from Headley, who appeared quite content with what he'd just heard. I was unable to speak and could feel myself beginning to shake. So, like a coward, I departed and headed for the car park.

Karen Morgan, a dermatologist, left at the same time. As she walked, she tripped slightly and was definitely a little pale. "Are you okay, Karen?" I asked. "You don't look well."

"Actually, no, I feel terrible," she slurred as she pushed through the door to the staircase. "I'm going home to bed. I think I'm having a migraine."

I should have intervened and offered her a ride home, but I didn't.

When I arrived home, Catherine was on the phone talking to Harvey. My brother had been on the phone to me for two hours the previous evening asking me how to tell our mother about his HIV. He wanted me to break the news to her.

I couldn't face speaking to him now and went upstairs for a shower. My daughter wandered in and asked me the question that upset both me and my wife, "Daddy, why are your boobies bigger than Mummy's?" She was always a little too honest.

Finished with the shower, I changed into clean clothes and went downstairs. Catherine had a new dress on. "You look lovely in that dress," I told her. "That colour really suits you."

"Oh, so you didn't like the dress I wore yesterday?"

H

On Tuesday, everyone was in a state of shock. Karen Morgan had driven off a perfectly straight road on her way home the previous night. The car had burst into flames on impact, and there was little remaining to identify her. She left behind a husband and three children.

Worse still, if one could judge from Jeremiah Foch's comments, she also left a twenty-two-week wait time from referral to being seen by the specialist, a breach of the targets that would show in the next accreditation visit. I was glad to be going away the next day to an international hematology meeting. But I wondered if her accident was my fault. I should have offered to take her home. I couldn't stop thinking about that; my patients in the afternoon clinic were all unhappy with my rather unfocused conversations.

Very little of Karen could be found. The police department made a half-hearted effort to do its paperwork. The rumour was that Inspector McAlister had been consulted but was watching darts on television and none of his colleagues dared disturb him. I received a phone call from one of the junior police officers, as did a few my colleagues, and I mentioned to him that Karen had suddenly felt unwell the evening of the accident. Three days later, the *Kilminster Journal* announced there were no suspicious circumstances. The coroner's verdict a few weeks later recorded accidental death.

8

A Conference Abroad

That same Tuesday, Catherine wanted us to put our money toward some new curtains. We went to a department store in town where she suggested that as well as getting curtains we buy a set of luxury suitcases with wheels. Her words were "Let's invest in some wheeled suitcases." In the history of financial advice, nobody had ever recommended investing in baggage. With these purchases, we'd already spent twice as much as anticipated, and my hope of a laptop computer once again faded.

However, Catherine decided the new suitcases were far too smart for me to travel with and instead sent me up to the attic to retrieve our old case, a hand-me-down from her mother that came with a fold-down metal trolley with two bungee cords to hold the bag in place. I'd seen several seasoned travellers with these and believed they made just as much sense as wheeled cases.

Since we'd first met, Catherine had insisted on packing my suitcases when I went away, so I was totally comfortable with that arrangement, especially because at least it guaranteed I'd be presentable whatever else went wrong on the trip.

On Wednesday, I was on my way to Madrid. In those days, pharmaceutical companies, better known as Big Pharma, pretty much paid the whole bill. They were delightfully corrupt, and it was hard to refuse a free flight, hotel, and meeting registration fees. In addition, of course, a week away from Oliver Michaels and Richard Headley was an extra bonus.

My wife had to stay behind to look after the children. The kids were all at school and were old enough to get themselves dressed and ready. Catherine worked as a part-time class assistant in the same school. Her mother was going to come down and stay for the rest of the week and the weekend, so I was happy she wouldn't be alone.

I drove to Gatwick Airport and parked in the long-stay car park. As usual, I arrived at the airport a little early, meaning three hours before the flight. I checked in and went in search of sustenance, finding a table at the back of a café. Reading the menu, I noticed I'd laid my wrist on some old ketchup, which now smeared the cuffs of my yellow sweater. I tried to wipe it off with a tissue with some sort of non-absorbent waxy coating but only succeeded in spreading the mark further. Giving up, I ordered a cheeseburger and fried onion rings from a young waitress with a ripe pustule on her left cheek. As she was bringing the food, my heart sank when I heard the grating Welsh twang of Oliver Michaels. *What the hell's he doing in an airport?* I thought. *I'm here to get away from work!*

Michaels barged into my table, causing my coffee to slop all over the place as he threw himself into the opposite seat, grinning at me with joy at our serendipitous meeting. I took a sip of what was left of my coffee and tried to appear delighted by his arrival. The coffee on the bottom of the cup dripped down my front, adding to my distress. When I ate a ring, a whole onion wormed its way out on the first bite, dripping grease onto my sweater.

With an extra roll of *r*'s and some Welsh alliteration, Michaels said, "Well, that's a rare rum drama, isn't it?"

"What is?"

"Karen, of course. Don't you think it's odd?"

"Sad, yes. Odd, I guess so, but I'm not really sure what happened. I heard she drove into a ditch." I didn't mention my conversation with Karen after the meeting two days earlier and got the impression he knew I hadn't offered her a lift and was blaming me.

What he did give me for certain was a meaningful look. "Mark my words, there's more to this than meets the eye," he insisted.

It turned out that Oliver was off to Frankfurt, Germany, for a different meeting. He didn't get any food or drink but sat in front of me as I ate, adding a certain flavour of decay to the cheeseburger. Then I noticed on the overhead electronic board that my plane was boarding from a gate about four miles from where we were sitting, so I rose hurriedly to leave.

"But I need to talk to you, Brian," Oliver said almost wistfully. "There's something going —"

"I'm sorry, Oliver, but I've got to go." And I rushed off. A better person would have stayed. A better person would have prevented what was to come. I chose fresh air instead.

I was sure I pulled a calf muscle as I marched purposefully toward

Gate 56. As I made my way, I was almost mowed down by a claret-covered electric car provided for the very elderly and those with disabilities. It was transporting a family of five — only one of whom vaguely fitted the eligibility criteria — and their luggage. Oddly, each of them seemed to have at least two oversized bags. When I finally reached the gate, the family was disembarking. The elderly lady sprang off, a bag in each hand. The other four seemed fitter than decathletes. Their luggage filled every spare overhead locker on the plane, so I had to stuff mine in the footwell, leaving me four square inches for my feet.

The suitcase trolley turned out to be a burden. My case was put in the hold, but I had to take the pull-along trolley onto the plane, packing it in a different compartment from my briefcase eight rows back because space was tight at my feet. When we arrived at Madrid's airport, I forgot the carrier, only remembering a few days later on the day of my planned return.

The journey to Madrid was otherwise uneventful except that when I arrived I had no idea which hotel I'd booked. Catherine was still at work, so I was unable to phone her to ask. I took a bus to the city centre, which was hot and busy and drifted around shops for two hours before I recalled that the whole itinerary was in my suitcase. I found a patch of pavement to open the case and found the documents. When I picked up the case, I discovered I'd put it in some of the city's ubiquitous dog muck and had no tissues to wipe it clean. The hotel wasn't in the city centre but near the airport. I took a taxi back along a now-familiar route and realized I'd already spent my foreign currency and wasn't even in my room yet.

Finding the conference centre and registering on Thursday took longer than anticipated. I now had a conference bag with nine pounds of mainly useless journals and invitations to symposia plus a pass for all the city transit services and a name tag to hang around my neck with my name spelled "Brain" rather than "Brian." I wanted to go home.

I was in Hall 2, a massive presentation area with seats that pressed on the sciatic nerve and an Italian man in front chatting at full volume to his friend. Behind me, someone was clicking the end of his pen. *Open, closed, open, closed, open, closed.* I shot him my meanest look, which was duly ignored. Then I rose and went to stand at the back of the room, already too irritated to learn anything.

We were required to attend a few national or international meetings per year. Thankfully, eighty percent of the cost of the meetings was funded by pharma companies, and despite a range of apparent compliance rules, they heavily influenced the content. International meetings were all the same: too big with too many people and always in rooms where one could barely see the screens usually somewhere on the horizon.

On the other hand, the companies gave out good pens and took us out to dinner. Tonight, in fact, we were going to meet up with the Pfizer team. Once again, I'd reconciled the long track record of dubious practices in favour of a three-course meal and the chance to meet with some old friends. We were due to meet in the lobby of one of the central hotels at 7:00 p.m. Despite getting there in plenty of time, they had all gone when I got there, so I ended up buying some crisps and chocolate milk and catching the subway back to my hotel.

I needed lunch on Friday and noticed a satellite symposium about to start on the latest amazing class of anticoagulants where lunch was free. Annoyingly, the time of the symposium was changed without publishing it. The speaker, Dave Green, was well known to me. We'd trained together. By year two, he was speaking to patients and colleagues as if his opinions were divinely given. After ten years, he'd backstabbed and lied his way to the academic zenith, which was ninety percent inhabited by genuine psychopaths who had the skill sets to assassinate colleagues on their way up the ladder.

As junior doctors in the 1980s, we were required to administer intravenous antibiotics at night, as if somehow after 5:00 p.m. nurses were no longer capable. This involved drawing up about twenty-five syringes of antibiotics and injecting them into lines inserted earlier in the day and hopefully still working. I never completed this task in fewer than forty-five minutes. Dave never took more than ten. I was four months into the post when I noticed Dave walking from patient to patient with a single giant syringe, giving each person one to two millilitres.

For six months, Dave, two other junior doctors, and I shared accommodation. On one occasion, Dave developed *pruritus ani*, better known as itchy bum. He was horrified to learn he had worms. The family doctor was quite insistent that all members of the household be treated. It made sense, and Dave already assumed his worms were a result of the poor hygiene of one of the other three. But he was unable to bring himself to discuss the problem. He bought a broad-spectrum horse wormer, strawberry flavour, from a farm shop on the edge of town, poured it into a strawberry mousse, and to this day, the other two were unaware of the cure that had been administered to them. I'd passed on the mousse because I was on another of my diets, which I started about every three months.

Somewhere between then and now, Dave had risen to the top, while I meanwhile had trickled along on a horizontal, or perhaps slightly downhill, trajectory. But Dave talked bullshit then and just as much now.

Now he rose to speak, and as required, presented a first slide of conflicts of interest — a list of pharma companies that had paid him, which was long and exhaustive. "I'm so dirty I'm clean," he said. I was sure a star on his tooth twinkled as he grinned and moved on to the next slide. At that point, I switched off to eat lunch but refocused as Dave reached his conclusion slide, that wonderful moment when one knew a lecture was nearly over.

His final words were presented with a well-practised flourish like a magician pulling one's watch out of another audience member's pocket: "If you aren't using Nixclotsa by this time next year, then you're negligent." The audience erupted, by which I mean the front two rows occupied by the sponsoring pharma team stood and clapped furiously, while everyone else in the room trailed out. I performed half a clap on my right thigh.

Big Pharma had invited me to dinner at a fish restaurant. When I arrived and peered through the window, I saw that everyone was already finishing their main course. They had clearly changed the time for dinner. Rather disgruntled, I took the subway back to my hotel and ate an apple I'd saved plus a stale ham-and-cheese roll from a vending machine in the lobby.

A day later, on Saturday, the competing pharma company put on its own satellite symposium, once again an hour earlier than advertised. I picked up a little white paper bag with a string handle, containing a sandwich, a bottle of water, a bag of crisps, and an apple, then found a seat at the back. Apparently, someone hadn't done his or her research. Here was Dave "I'm So Dirty I'm Clean" Green with the slides other than the results graphs. But he did have a new conclusion: "If you're not using Nothrombo by this time next year, then you're negligent." *Or maybe,* I thought, *make up your own mind and don't do as Dave tells you. And remember, every guideline you read is written by a group with the conflict of interest of massive pharma income.*

As I shuffled out of the presentation hall with the aim of finding some free pens for my kids, I felt I was too young to express so much contempt at corrupt colleagues. Nevertheless, I was feeling happy with myself because I'd only eaten two-thirds of the packet of crisps, calculated the calories saved, and credited that to my final fitness. "And I'm such a hypocrite," I said to myself, smiling as I found some note pads in the shape of red blood cells and a squeezy stress ball labelled NOTHROMBO. I used my Nothrombo pen to devise my Fifth Rule:

BRIAN'S FIFTH RULE

This rule applies mainly to academic key opinion leaders but extends to all fields of medicine. *The more certainty you hear from your doctor the more likely they're talking garbage.* If pharma has paid the expert, then double-down on your doubt. If the phrase "statistically significant" is made, ask whether that equates to "clinically significant."

I realized then that my fifth rule applied not just to medicine but to all aspects of life. Maybe it should read: "Beware of anyone preaching with certainty." I'd work on that.

The afternoon sessions were part of the "State of the Art" series. The problem was that the conference was in English but the speaker was Greek. He wasn't told how to use the microphone, so most of the time he looked left and right at the audience and nothing could be heard. Every so often he leaned forward toward the microphone, resulting in a loud blurt of unintelligible noise. Such were European meetings. It was rare to go home with new knowledge.

I was drifting off again and felt that my continuous professional development might be achieved by reflecting on the things that annoyed me.

Annoying Things

- Excessive cheerfulness.
- People who get off a bus, then stop to chat, which happened upon arrival from the hotel to the conference centre where four Russians blocked the rest of the coach from disembarking.
- People who think they're hippies, particularly the man near me now in his sixties with a ponytail and flip-flops.
- People who quote *Monty Python*, especially the guy at breakfast who recited the whole "Dead Parrot" sketch.
- Men with tenuous connections to Scotland wearing kilts at formal balls.

- Scottish men wearing kilts.
- Personalized number plates. Why was I thinking about Richard Headley? And why had the new cardiologist paid a fortune for H4RT? And do all the plates at a cardiology conference feature variations of H4RT?

When I glanced up, I spotted a couple of French guys gorging on free food, so I added:

- Eating with an open mouth.
- Bad personal hygiene.

I was happy with the list so far and folded the paper carefully, eyeing a woman enviously who had a laptop. At home I had a desktop computer but hadn't saved enough money for a laptop yet.

After the Saturday conference, I met up with a couple of colleagues who suggested we go into town, which we did, quaffing three lagers each before moving on to various plates of tapas. Annoyingly, we hadn't tagged up with a drug rep, so I actually had to pay for my own beers and tapas. Luckily, there was a meal arranged for 7:30 p.m. with a meeting point at the five-star hotel where the reps were staying.

However, somehow my wallet had been stolen. My colleagues were gracious, but I knew they likely felt the same as I would in a similar situation. So when I returned to the hotel, I had to call Catherine and pay an extortionate rate to get her to cancel my credit card.

"But I've got to put the children to bed," she complained. "It's all right for you to swan off with your mates on the other side of the world, leaving me with the children and two dogs. I've already had to spend two hours at the vet. Ben has another ear infection. We've got some new antibiotics — £80."

I did a quick calculation. I'd had £50 in my wallet and the same in Spanish currency. Eighty for the dog. And about £100 for a jacket I'd left in a restaurant the night before. I felt slightly sick and wanted to go home.

In the end, Catherine and I agreed I'd cancel the card.

After that conversation, I headed back on the subway for the evening dinner, but upon arriving, discovered the group had once again left. So, feeling deflated and slightly unwanted, I returned to my hotel for an evening by myself.

The phone bill presented as I checked out the next morning was equivalent to £140. This was taken out of the deposit, luckily, since all I had to my name now were a few coins in my pockets.

At that point, I realized I hadn't put my watch forward an hour to the local time, and that the reason I'd missed every evening meal was because I'd arrived late for every single one. As it turned out, I'd also booked the return flight twenty-four hours too early.

I'd spent every last note and coin in the airport shop on a book, a packet of peanuts, and a can of Coke and was pretty happy not having to return home with foreign currency that would spend the next decade in my sock drawer. For the family, I used my last traveller's cheque on presents for them. Then, at the check-in counter, the terrible news was revealed. With a rush of adrenaline, I discovered I had no money for phone calls, no money for a new ticket, a wife meeting me at the airport in two hours, and as I picked up my suitcase, recalled I had no fancy fold-down carrier.

Borrowing some money from a conference delegate from Oldham, I promised to pay her back in a few days and was able to contact Catherine's mother. My wife was already on her way to the airport to collect me, so there was no way to reach her.

I lugged my case and conference bag to a seat in the terminal and sat down, too depressed to work out what to do next. I had no money and no ticket. I knew the doghouse was truly to be my home for a week or so.

When I called home again, I learned that Catherine's mother had found me a flight to the Luton airport and paid for it. I could collect the ticket at the airline desk and would be flying back in only eighteen hours.

In the air and on my way home, I was jammed in a middle seat with someone each side of me, and for thirty minutes there was a subtle unspoken battle for real estate on the armrest. The chief steward then asked if there was a doctor on board.

The best action in cases like this was to keep quiet. There were always two or three doctors on a plane and always one who believed he or she was the physician of the year. Alarmingly, though, my hubris took over and I eagerly identified myself. While I was ushered down the plane, I asked myself whether this would be a heart attack, or epilepsy, or some other acute emergency. What I got was a redheaded twelve-year-old boy with airsickness.

As I reached the boy, he vomited again into the aisle and all over my lower legs. His mother was next to him and passed me a white bag full of semi-digested pizza Napoli with Coke. I felt fairly redundant but tried hard to assume an air of gravitas while offering fatuous advice. Then I returned to my seat, at which point I realized I was still clutching the bag of vomit.

I held on to the bag until we disembarked and carried it up the plane to give to a member of the cabin crew. But they were all engaged in trying to wheel a patient out on a narrow wheelchair. I ended up dumping the vomit on the counter of the airline near the gate and was spotted by a member of the cabin crew, who marched over and told me I was disgusting and inconsiderate.

While I was being admonished, I noticed the pukey child walk past with his mother. I never again raised my hand when asked if a doctor was on board.

BRIAN'S SEVENTH RULE

When you set yourself up as a hero, expect vomit on your shoe. This rule clearly has development potential, but I think the essence is there for us to work on. It's akin to the proverb "Pride comes before a fall," but I felt mine was much more late twentieth century.

There was one incident that perked me up a little on the journey home. At the luggage carousel, everyone was pushed up to the belt, waiting for their cases and not allowing me even the vaguest glimpse to see if mine was coming. Where the carousel turned back on itself, a seven-year-old ginger-haired boy with a mullet and an earring actually sat on its edge. The mother called out, "Ludo, come back from there," but the toxic child ignored her only to have his fingers pinched a few seconds later by a case as it rounded the corner. Joy of joys, it was my own that had done it! I had a spring in my step for the next ten minutes, though on reflection I did wonder if my happy response to this episode made me a bad person.

Catherine drove to the airport to pick me up, but it was the "Drive of Disapproval" for the first ten minutes before she said, "Brian, you do this every time," with a huge smile. So, for some reason, I wasn't in the doghouse but returned home a hero, distributing pharma-sponsored loot among the children. That night I slept well, vowing never to attend another European conference.

9

The Emancipation of Neville

In February 1998, Sally White was a force and not a positive one. Something more malevolent. Unyielding. Threatening. Effective in terms of clinic throughput, though not when measured in terms of patient satisfaction. She generally took a non-negotiable stance with patients who left perhaps with the right treatment but rarely happy. If not for a face set in a constant impatient frown, she could have been an attractive woman. However, she also had a peculiar gait that made it appear as if someone had inserted a pineapple in her rectally. She wore trousers so tight there was never any ambiguity about her genital anatomy, which added to the general sense of alarm most people felt as she approached.

Her husband, Neville Botham, hadn't made his fortune from emus yet. Three had survived to adulthood, while the cassowary remained in a smaller enclosure. Similarly, the alpacas had so far only produced enough wool for one baby sock and had cost £3,000 in veterinary bills.

They say people look like their pets. The cassowary had an uncanny resemblance to Sally, or so her husband thought. For his part, Neville had developed an air of melancholy, his wispy beard dangling sadly from his defeated chin. He washed even less and exuded a bitter odour that matched his bitter life. The one positive, I was told, was that Sally refused to consider sex. Since she had induced irreversible impotence in her husband, this no doubt felt like a win-win situation for him and he looked for solace in spending hours each day mowing the field with a ride-on lawn mower, having been banned by Sally from getting a tractor, or browsing educational journals searching for a local job teaching geography. He almost found one, but Sally forbade him from applying, since he had multiple chores on their small holding that she expected to be completed efficiently.

Neville told me that he pondered daily how life might have taken a different turn if he'd had more courage and stood up for himself like a man when three years earlier Sally unexpectedly told him they were to get married. He couldn't even understand why, since there hadn't been a spark of romance or love from day one. While not really a committed Christian, Neville had attended a Bible class for a few terms at university and developed a friendship with a very earnest girl doing a PhD on the change in weaving techniques across the Roman Empire, 200 to 700 AD. He was entranced by her and was trying to pluck up the courage to ask her out for a coffee and toasted teacake at the Copper Kettle, a small café in a narrow cobbled street near St. Mary's Church. But before he could do that, he met Sally, who was in her final year of medical school, through a mutual friend. Even now, Neville couldn't explain how he ended up married in a register office only seven months after an uncomfortable courtship.

The marriage was consummated at a Holiday Inn in York, with Sally simultaneously watching an episode of *Antiques Roadshow*, but the passion died on that same evening. She told him they'd stay together, and he then loyally followed her through her training.

One day, Neville related to me later, he was trying to lift a roll of barbed wire from his car when it dropped on the back of his foot, passing through Wellington boots covered in alpaca dung and causing six deep puncture wounds. He called Sally, who of course refused to talk to him. Then he phoned his family doctor, who asked him to come in for a tetanus shot. However, upon seeing the wound, his doctor sent him to the urgent care centre where he sat on a chair waiting his turn. Jeremiah Foch passed through and wandered over to say hello. He promised to try to expedite things because Sally had just called demanding to know if Neville had prepared her supper and wondered "who was going to lock up the birds and alpacas."

And thus began the chain of events, starting with a roll of barbed wire, that led to the emancipation of Neville, as he later dramatically referred to it in years to come.

H

Sally hadn't been happy all day at work. Her colleagues at the hospital knew that was hardly anything new. As reconstructed after the event, one evening, she arrived home from work at 7:00 p.m. The farmhouse was dark and empty. Neville had called to say he was still waiting to be seen and the wait time was estimated at another three hours.

She put on her Barber jacket and Hunter wellies and stepped out the door. There was a light frost already stiffening the grass. She considered leaving the animals to Neville, but the alpacas sometimes disturbed their neighbour, Angus McAlister, an ill-tempered police inspector with whom she was already in dispute over their mutual hedge. They'd reached the point that whenever the cars met on the narrow road to the property, neither of them volunteered to reverse and sat there waiting for one to weaken. Sally was pleased that it was rarely her who chose to back up.

Grabbing a flashlight whose beam lasted for about ten steps before dimming yellow and then turning off, she threw it angrily to the ground and guided herself toward the stable and bird enclosure. It was cloudy and there was little light. The alpacas were all in the stable, so it was straightforward to swing the door closed and bolt it. The emus were a little stupider and required some herding to get them to go where they were needed. Sally stepped into their enclosure, holding a long broom in one hand and a dustbin lid in the other, and started clicking at them irritably to get them to move. It was dark, cold, and the emus weren't responding to her orders.

There was a shuffling, and for a moment, she thought she glimpsed a shadow running toward her. She tried to defend herself with the dustbin lid but felt a terrible blow and a burning, tearing pain in her abdomen and a wet feeling running down her legs. And then she felt nothing. Because she was dead.

H

Neville found Sally three hours later. There was a hideous expression of final recognition on her face. Claudette, the cassowary, stood calm and silent on the far side of the enclosure, but the sequence of events was indisputable. Claudette had always been irritable and difficult, more so even than Sally herself, and had disembowelled Sally with one kick before contentedly returning to pecking at the ground. The police agreed that it was an accidental death.

Angus McAlister, the police inspector, arrived along with his deputy, who appeared to be Eastern European because she had a look that said she'd kill you slowly and enjoy it. Rumour had it there had been an occasion several years earlier when the deputy had let the side down and briefly smiled; her family had called a doctor in case she was mentally ill.

McAlister, had been on the wrong end of Sally's wrath over a dispute about a row of Leyland cypress trees. He'd also lost several staring stand-offs from his car, which usually ended with him reversing to a gap in the hedge. Sally had arranged for Neville to plant the trees the afternoon they'd taken possession of the property, but her husband had put them on the wrong side of the property line and they'd already grown three feet over McAlister's land. And then mysteriously all of the trees had died over a two-week period when the inspector was away visiting his parents in Glasgow.

Sally had suspected foul play and so started the boundary dispute that began with a further planting of more mature trees, which also perished bafflingly, once again when Angus was away. Most recently, a fence had been erected, and both Sally and Angus were relieved that they didn't have to glimpse each other, apart from when they met in the lane to the properties.

H

The inspector wasn't his usual dour self at Sally's crime scene. He was worse. His mirthless Scottish wife had unexpectedly rejected his gift of a tent, formerly used to hide dead bodies from eager cameras but no longer needed. McAlister had brought it home and arranged a trip to a camp-site close to the Wardlaw Mausoleum ten miles from Inverness. His wife felt that this part of Scotland would suck the soul from the most ardent nationalist, and to lie there in the murder tent would be the nadir of her life. McAlister had never heard of a nadir, so was less offended than he might have been.

Gazing down at Sally, McAlister asked in his slightly terrifying Glaswegian accent, "Who would have ever thought she'd finally meet her match?" Given the situation, the comment seemed a little tactless, though Neville quite agreed and nodded approvingly. "Aye, she could be a total fucking bitch," added the inspector. "I think if your ostrich hadn't done it, then there were plenty of people who would've had a bash."

"She's a cassowary," said Neville.

Angus looked at him blankly. He was more interested in getting home to watch the Winter Olympics.

Claudette was transferred south to Paignton Zoo, and Neville put the farm up for sale before the funeral even took place. He sold it quickly, the emus and alpacas included in the sale price.

Life once again seemed altogether finer at Kilminster Hospital, though the increased wait time was noted in a memo at the next staff meeting. Strangely, nobody was found available to write an obituary or say a few words on Sally's behalf.

10

Mum Knew

Many moons ago when there were no cars, people might have travelled by horse. Even longer ago, they might have written with quills. And hard though it was to believe, there was a time in the 1990s when if people needed something, they went to shops to buy it.

At the beginning of April 1998, Catherine and I received an unexpected tax rebate and discussed whether to buy a new lawn mower or a videocassette player. We'd made it a policy to be financially imprudent and rarely considered saving when we could be spending. In a wild moment of compromise, we decided to buy both and got the video player from an electronics store on the high street, which closed down four days later. I'd read a review about a different machine, but while I was looking at it, the shop assistant wandered over and said, "That's a great choice. I've got the same machine at home."

I glanced at him. He had three earrings, dirty hair, and sounded as if he came from the north of England. I pictured him with a whippet and a pint of brown ale, watching a video, and immediately began to feel revulsion. I did have insight into some of the misanthropic thoughts that governed my life but was quite horrified that this fellow thought his personal choice was congruent with my own. So, I had to search for a different machine. I'd done the same three months earlier at the bed shop when the same words were used over a mattress, and the thought of the three-hundred-pound bed salesman on the mattress had once again prompted me to make an alternative choice.

We next went to buy some blank tapes so we could record from the television. Then we set up an account at Blockbuster and rented *Titanic* to watch that night. When we raced home to set it all up, we discovered to our dismay that I had the wrong leads to plug into the television. So we left the system ready to go and hurried back into town to get the right connectors. Successful in that mission, we went to the do-it-yourself store on the ring road to get a lawn mower. By the end of all this activity, I had that glow developed between the purchase and the credit card bill.

The lawn mower came in a large box but rather irritatingly had to be assembled. However, I managed the ordeal, with only two nuts and bolts unaccounted for, then remembered we had to buy fuel. I drove off again, now tired of the journey into town, to purchase a red plastic container for the petrol, and thence to the station to fill it up. Back home, I filled the mower. In fact, it overflowed, but I didn't notice until later when I saw the asphalt on the driveway melting. I decided on an urgent mowing of the lawn, but within five minutes I hit a metal fence post I'd laid out four weeks earlier, somehow damaging the drive shaft of the mower, which was now totally unserviceable.

In the forty minutes it took to wreck the mower, our youngest child inserted a peanut butter sandwich into the VHS machine, which now made a constant whirring sound. Although I extracted most of the sandwich, the recording heads were covered with peanut butter. We decided to give *Titanic* a go, but within four seconds, the tape jammed in the machine so that we could neither play nor remove it.

H

On Easter Sunday, we drove up to my mother's house. My father had died a few years earlier, and she lived alone in a large house she was reluctant to heat, so Catherine and the kids were always a little hesitant to stay over. Hence, we chose to go up and back the same day. My younger daughter had brought her teddy, Nobby, which took up undue space in the car. We'd barely arrived when I saw my mother's small poodle, Nonny, trying to have sex with Nobby. Nonny and Nobby — a love made in heaven.

There were several jobs that needed doing around the house for Mum, and we got cracking with these while lunch was being made. Mum had set up an Easter egg hunt in the garden for the children who joyfully harvested the chocolate. Then she asked us to help move a wardrobe in her bedroom to a different wall. While doing this, I couldn't help but notice some tablets on her dressing table and quite rudely felt I had to know what they were. I read the word *tamoxifen*, a hormone pill used for breast cancer, and was immediately confused. Why would she keep this from us? Weren't we close enough that she could share it? When was she diagnosed? So many questions flooded through my mind.

We finished moving the wardrobe, and I went downstairs to the kitchen and asked Mum directly, "How long have you been on tamoxifen?"

She stared at me. "You've got enough to worry about without fretting about me."

"But this isn't a small thing. When was it diagnosed? Did you have any surgery?"

"I had a lumpectomy three years ago, and things were fine until last winter when my oncologist told me the cancer had spread to my bones."

I knew we hadn't visited Mum for more than four months and felt guilty, as rightly I should. "You should still have told me."

"Like you should have told me about Harvey?"

I froze. *Not my news to give*, I thought, but foolishly replied, "What are you talking about?"

"I know. I'm not stupid."

Did she mean about the HIV? "That he's gay?"

She actually laughed. "Oh, for God's sake, I knew that when he was twelve. And I knew he was being foolish whenever he went away with Uncle Paul. I just want him to feel he can tell me he has AIDS."

And there it was. Harvey hadn't told her, and she thought he was about to die. We had a good chat about the difference between AIDS and being HIV positive. I told her that I now had a lot of patients who were HIV positive, and it currently seemed as if one could live a long life with the infection.

The children were playing in the orchard, so we were able to set things straight, and Catherine invited Mum down to stay with us the following weekend. I promised to ask Harvey to join us. Despite this, lunch was excellent, and as we were putting everything back in the car, my mother asked, "Do you want my old lawn mower? I bought a new one on Friday."

H

On Saturday, April 10, Harvey told me he was in a "holding pattern," as he described it. Meanwhile, in the space of a week, my mother seemed diminished, though that was perhaps because I now saw her as a dying human being instead of a tour de force. But the spark appeared to have gone.

I recalled being in Greece when I was eighteen when I dropped my new camera, which I'd had for four days, into the Aegean. I watched it disappear from sight, glinting occasionally until it was gone. My mother's very essence was doing the same, sinking away from me perceptibly, uncontrollably, and inevitably. I could see the drama of her demise mapped out ahead of us: increasing dependence, intensifying pain, and the long wait everybody went through but didn't want to talk about. I found myself hoping for her sudden death, then experienced guilt for even thinking that.

Was I hoping this for her to avoid suffering? Or were my thoughts selfish? It made me feel guilty that my mother's breast cancer had turned into a problem for me and how it would impact my own life. Meanwhile, Catherine didn't seem to have any of these wicked thoughts and had already developed a comprehensive plan of support.

The weekend weather matched my mood: grey, damp, depressing.

"Oh, for God's sake, Brian this isn't about you," said Catherine.

I decided it was time to reacquaint myself with the Bible, and I suspect that for a while I was quite difficult to live with. Catherine, at a later date, told me I'd always been that way. I even went to church, but halfway through the service, while my mind was elsewhere, the vicar said something and the whole congregation turned around and shook hands with everybody in front and behind, muttering something about the peace of the Lord. I wasn't familiar with this, and my misanthropy was multiplied when I unexpectedly found myself shaking hands with people I had no desire to touch. I spotted Mrs. Duncan from the League of Friends beaming at me as if I were a new recruit, and my mind reeled with memories of middle-aged women with crowned teeth and ridiculous hats singing the descant to "Oh Come All Ye Faithful." I couldn't get out fast enough.

Clearly, church wasn't resonating with my mood, but at least I could make more of an effort to visit my mother in her large, cold, lonely house. I also noticed that my own family was collecting illnesses, that I was becoming more empathetic with patients, and ruefully realized I'd probably been far worse than I'd even acknowledged in terms of developing rapport.

11

Revenge of the Black Snake

In the past four months, three new colleagues had joined the Trust and one had died, eviscerated by her own cassowary. Since Sally White had died three months earlier, a Tuesday morning clinic slot was up for grabs. Several consultants made bids for this clinic, which at first sight seemed philanthropic. Sadly not. The bidders were currently working Friday clinics and wished to drop those to allow them to spend that day at the local private hospital.

Apparently, there was a dearth of available cardiologists, so the new appointment was put on hold until a few more trainees were available. This boosted Richard Headley's private income considerably but pushed the cardiology wait time from twenty-two to thirty-two weeks, resulting in a regional Health Authority red flag on the whole hospital, with an accreditation visit just around the corner.

The medical staff meeting agenda was long, making dismal reading:

Agenda: Medical Staff Meeting, Monday, April 20, 1998, 5:00 p.m.

Regrets: Daniel Collins.
Minutes of last meeting.
Review of outpatient space.
Cardiology vacancies.
Wait-time initiative.
Junior doctor new educational style. Problem-based learning.
Consultant dining room, date of closure for management block
    expansion.
Hospital records system training.
New annual leave rules — management sign-off required (Miss Dove
    from HR will present).
Any other business.

We were barely halfway through when it became obvious the meeting was likely to overrun until about 7:00 p.m. unless I could drop in the opportunity to carry items over to give us time for measured reflection, a phrase that was usually successful.

Jeremiah Foch next explained that an informal survey of hospital staff had confirmed that most felt it was inappropriate for the consultants to have their own dining room. Consensus was that they should eat like everybody else in the main canteen where the managers had already chosen to remove the barriers separating the staff from the patients and their families.

"I wasn't surveyed, Jerry," said Headley.

"It's Jeremiah" was his reply.

"Sorry, Mr. Foch."

The outpatient space was to be reviewed, and I was to go from two clinic rooms to one, which would allow the building of a new block for the managers' offices.

A new handbook of assessment for junior doctors had been produced, and the associate dean from the medical school was scheduled to visit next week for a half-day workshop to teach us how to do this, which resulted in the late cancellation of clinics for eight of us. The essence was that however useless you were as a junior doctor, you couldn't actually fail to progress because failing a student reflected on the supervisor. That seemed marginally Orwellian to me.

The new assessment tool had one clear effect: if a junior doctor was useless and couldn't be let loose on humanity, the best thing to do was to give him or her a clear pass and move the problem to a new post. The alternative was to highlight a deficiency, which of course would be the supervisor's fault, and recommend a remediation plan. In so doing, the floodgates were opened to litigation for having the temerity to doubt the perfection of the doctor in question. Extending the logic, it was clear that most medical schools considered their selection criteria for choosing students were close to perfect.

My own insight was that we were doing a great job of selecting competitive sociopaths at least fifteen percent of the time. My experience of medical school was enough to show me there were some truly wonderful people and some truly terrible ones in every year. Five years later, most would have been indoctrinated into the medical culture.

Nigel Robinson wanted to speak during the "any other business" section. He was simply boring. There was nothing specifically to dislike about him other than a constant odour of raw onion, but most normal humans treated him like Ebola. They avoided too much time in his company. At some point in his life, he presumably decided he needed to be funny. Sadly, he had no comic genius or native wit. Instead, he had an irritating ability to raise his eyebrows and an astonishing inability to master the double entendre. Being in his company was like living in a 1970s sitcom, but less funny. There were few sentences he could utter without adding "as the actress said to the bishop," or "say no more." He was a consultant in care of the elderly, so I hoped for his patients' sakes they couldn't hear him or his feeble innuendos.

None of this was helped by the fact that as a child somebody must have touched Nigel with the ugly stick several times. He had the most bizarrely horizontal teeth, which were always visible and surrounded by cherry-red lips that constantly had a shiny gleam of saliva. While I was perhaps being rather unfair to raise something over which he had no control, I contended that it added to the overall sense of annoyance when he inevitably stood in a meeting, since he was incapable of discussing anything without doing so. A gag and a paper bag would have made him far more likable.

He was presenting a case for something tedious on his ward, some sort of catheter, or maybe industrial clippers, or an angle grinder for thick, horny toenails. I wasn't sure I was listening as he droned on. Finally, he finished with "And we'll need some lubricating jelly, nudge-nudge, wink-wink."

This was what it had come to. Four of my colleagues actually chuckled, the patronizing kind tinged with "I hope he doesn't suggest we go for a drink. I'll do a two-second laugh and smile, but I mustn't catch his eye."

Nigel was proud to be the medical staff comedian and smiled his appreciation at the imagined applause.

As for the rest of the meeting, I couldn't recall anything. I still have the notes I took, which consisted of drawings of three-dimensional dice and arrows, so perhaps I lost track. The weekend had left me exhausted, and my mind kept wandering back to the lawn mower, the video player, and my mum's breast cancer.

H

At 6:15 p.m. on Tuesday, most of the staff had gone home. I had a couple of grant applications to finish and was heading back to my office, which had now been moved to the pathology floor one level underground. The move, in fact, had proven far more convenient to me, since much of my day involved reviewing blood films under a microscope in the hematology and biochemistry labs on the same floor. So, I was pleased to be downstairs. My previous office had been located in the original old building where ventilation was poor and there was always a vague odour of decay, which I was sure visitors thought exuded from me or my secretary.

I was just getting over a cold and needed to sneeze. There were no tissues in my pocket, so I sneezed into my hand and was wiping it on the inside of my pocket when who should I meet but Colin Marks. What incredible luck! I shook his hands warmly. "Evening, Colin. I didn't think you knew this floor existed. Are you lost?"

"Uh … oh," he stammered." Hi, Brian, uh, no, I was actually just looking for Will Barker. I … I need to review some histology."

"On one of your privately insured patients, judging by the time."

"Well, as it happens, yes, but that's a little harsh. Pint?"

"Sorry, I really can't. I need to get the girls to Brownies as soon as I'm home."

"Actually, now that you're here, I … I was going to ask you for some … some advice. You see, I … I tested my blood count and it's a little on the low side."

"How low's low, Colin?"

He showed me his results written on the back of a cigarette packet. I saw that he was severely anemic. We performed the usual consultant-to-consultant informal appointment standing in the corridor, with no physical examination, of course.

"Looks like you're losing blood from somewhere, mate," I told him. "This is your territory. I bet there's an ulcer or something in your bowel. Don't you need an endoscopy? Maybe the whisky's catching up with you?"

"To be honest, old man, I think it's coming from the other end. The toilet bowl this morning looked as if I'd poured a bottle of Merlot down it."

"That's not good. It looks to me as if you need a colonoscopy." I grinned. "And that means getting Mary Taylor to do it. I think that might help her get rid of whatever it is that's been up between the two of you for the past two years. Maybe twenty minutes with the black snake shoved up your backside and she'll forgive you anything!" I think he felt I was being a little less earnest and sympathetic than he'd anticipated.

"Actually, no, I ... I don't think she ever will. I'd literally rather have my leg amputated than let her anywhere near me. I'll have to get referred out of town, which is why I ... I came to see you. I just wanted to know you agreed this looks like blood loss and not some sort of bone-marrow failure."

"Shouldn't that come from your GP?" I asked.

"She fired me recently. I'm currently between doctors. And nobody seems in a hurry to take me on for some reason. I ... I think Mary may have told a few folks what happened between us."

"And what exactly was that?"

"Uh, oh, you really don't need to know."

Maybe because you're such a wanker, I thought, but all I did was nod my sympathy and concern. In fact, despite his numerous flaws, at least with Colin I knew what I was getting, not like some of the snakes I worked with. But I was reluctant to write a referral letter elsewhere based on a corridor consult and told him so.

Then I headed on to my office, smiling at Nancy, Richard Headley's current wife, who worked as one of the administration staff in the pathology department. She hurried past on her way to the staff car park.

When I got home, it was a little late, and Catherine had taken the children to Brownies. They had left the house half an hour before I got home. I had to wait for somebody to turn around in my driveway before I could park on the front drive. We had a new springer spaniel puppy, which was sitting at the door as I strode in, seemingly forlorn, so I grabbed his lead and took him for a walk while Catherine and the children were gone. As I proceeded up the street, there was an enormous explosion and an orange fireball rising into the sky from behind my house. I was only fifty or so yards away and felt the warmth of the fireball as I stared at the sky with incomprehension. I didn't appreciate quite yet that the explosion wasn't *behind* my house. More specifically, it was the *back* of my house. I had just bought a laptop and recall, rather oddly, that my first thought was whether it would be damaged.

I rushed to knock on a house three up from my own, but nobody answered. Then I went next door where a rather intimidating woman from Liverpool appraised me as if I were an arsonist as I urged her to phone the fire brigade. In the end, she called her husband, who walked out to the road, gazed at my house, then ran in to dial 999. It had already been several minutes, and my laptop was bound to be burned, I realized.

H

I took the day off on Wednesday. The house had been extensively damaged, and we'd have to move into Harvey's house for an unspecified length of time. The fire brigade needed to conduct a forensic examination of the property, and there were insurance claims to be filed. Catherine had left the gas on in the oven, according to the investigator, though she insisted she couldn't have done so because she hadn't cooked that day. The investigator's report clearly showed she had, and at one point., he called her "my dear," which could easily have resulted in a broken mandible for him. The claims adjuster at the insurance company was delighted not to have to accept Catherine's version, leaving us needing to apply for a mortgage extension prior to enduring a few months of renovating work.

My laptop hadn't survived, of course, but the front half of the house was apparently in better shape than we'd expected, since the kitchen was in an extension at the back of the property, which had taken most of the force of the explosion. A large blue tarpaulin was draped over the roof. We had the clothes we were wearing at the time; the girls went to school the next day in their Brownie uniforms.

On Thursday, I had to go into work, though I should have taken a week or two off. We had a hematology meeting, and then I was supposed to do an hour's junior doctor teaching. About to head off toward the medical education centre, I encountered running in the opposite direction two medical students, the cardiac arrest team, and of all people, Richard Headley.

"You have to come and see this, mate!" Headley yelled as he flew past.

Mildly intrigued, I turned and followed the crowd toward the endoscopy suite. As I reached it, Larry Yen emerged. I'd never seen him with any sort of expression on his face before, and now he was also sweating. "Are you all right, Larry?" I asked.

"My God, I don't know what I'm feeling. Don't go in there."

Of course, I didn't heed his advice, pushed through the double doors, and heard which way I needed to go — the endoscopy room. It was small and contained four medical students; four junior medical staff; Jeremiah Foch and his sidekick, each clutching their clipboards; and two endoscopy nurses. I barged my way through to see a patient had fallen off the endoscopy table, sustaining a bad head wound as he landed.

Wait!

No!

It can't be!

And what the hell is that? I thought as I tried to piece together the scene before me.

Headley had a colossal grin on his face. "Well, at least he found his colonic polyp." Richard pointed at the image on the endoscopy video screen.

At our feet lay a very dead Colin Marks, still clutching the colonoscope, which he'd clearly self-guided all the way to the descending colon without sedation to avoid the ministrations of his colleagues. As I gazed at the corpse, I felt a little concerned that I wasn't as distressed as I should have been at his demise.

At this point, the cardiac arrest team arrived. The body had clearly been dead for at least three hours, but inexplicably the team rolled the corpse onto its back to commence cardiac massage. Headley, prompted by Jeremiah, told one of the medical students to hold the colonoscope. Jeremiah was concerned lest it get damaged and worsen the budgetary bottom line.

"Don't worry about the scope, Jezzer," Richard said.

"It's Jeremiah," replied "Jezzer" indignantly.

"Sorry, Mr. Foch, but there are worse nicknames I can think of."

There then ensued about five minutes of desultory cardiopulmonary resuscitation by an arrest team that clearly didn't have its heart in it until Headley declared we'd tried hard enough and could call the time of death. In a rare moment of sympathy, he also decided we should term this a heart attack on the death certificate and spare the family embarrassment.

I suspected, in fact, that despite Richard's love of media attention, he wasn't convinced his profile would be raised by standing in front of the hospital entrance and describing to the local news team how a consultant had managed to expire in such a way. At the moment, he was substituting for Margaret Crocker as medical director because she was on stress leave after one of her Yorkshire terriers had developed colitis and ruined her Persian carpet.

At this point, I should add that I sympathized with Crocker's dog, since colitis was no laughing matter, though it was thanks to a loose stool that I took up fishing as a hobby. I caught a train to London for a meeting at the College of Physicians some time ago. I was there three hours early, so I decided to walk from the station in Paddington into town, then north afterward to get to the meeting, which was at the edge of Regent's Park.

The night before, Catherine and I had been out for an Indian meal, and as I set off from the station, I felt a mild abdominal twinge of disapproval. I continued striding, but every six or seven minutes, I got a further painful twinge. Nevertheless, I ploughed on toward Oxford Street, cut through Mayfair, and was on my way to Soho when the discomfort changed from mild to some fairly impressive abdominal colicky pains every two minutes. By the time I was in Chinatown, the situation took a dramatic turn for the worse, and I began to use muscles the Yorkshire terrier had lacked to avoid my chicken jalfrezi from exacting its revenge.

I now had constant abdominal pain, and my gait had changed somewhat. Psychologically, I gave myself three minutes to get to the toilet, then spotted a large bookshop ahead. I waddled through the door and desperately searched for a floor plan to find the washrooms, which were on the next level as it turned out. There was an escalator. I could do this. My mind gave me one minute to make it. I reached the top of the escalator, immediately spotted the sign for the toilets, and limped, no doubt looking like Quasimodo by now. But as I approached, to my horror, I noticed a yellow sign telling me the toilet was closed.

What happened next wasn't something that gave me pride. I could only apologize to the person who discovered the result. Seeing there was a staff toilet next to the closed one, I tried the door, and to my huge relief, it was open! I burst in, slammed the door shut while simultaneously undoing my belt and button, and started to relax the various muscles keeping the deluge in place.

Then I noticed two things: first, this wasn't a toilet but a storeroom for magazines; second, there was a pile of periodicals on the floor in the corner. The rest of the details could be guessed, other than to confirm that this was my first introduction to *Trout and Salmon* magazine.

Afterward, I felt pretty guilty, but not enough to confess to anyone. However, I did buy a magazine when I returned to the ground floor, with a free fishing fly included. And on the train home that evening I began my lifelong passion for fly fishing. So perhaps my ordeal had been ordained.

H

In a mere three-month period, we'd lost three colleagues and I'd lost half my house and my new laptop. I found it hard to feel an appropriate sense of loss over either Sally or Colin, though I was rather sad about the computer. I took the morning off for a Marks & Spencer shopping bonanza but had to be back at the hospital by noon. My purchases included a pair of brown dress trousers and a cream-coloured shirt, which I thought gave me a James Bond–like image.

On Friday, the managers at the hospital organized an urgent staff meeting over lunch to discuss the unexpected loss of Colin Marks. After discovering the body, Dr. Yen had finally been stimulated into having a personality and actually communicating with his colleagues. He urged restraint and respect regarding the mode of Colin's death.

Richard told us, "I changed my mind. At the squash club last night, I let them know what happened to poor Colin. Let's face it, nothing in Kilminster is ever a secret for long, so why bother keeping it under wraps?"

Derek Newby, the recently appointed third gastroenterologist, asked, "Will there be an additional honorarium if I stand in as head of the GI Division?" He was like a cartoon character with dollar signs in the eyes because he had inherited overnight a lucrative private practice and a better office.

Mary Taylor was on stress leave.

Jeremiah asked, "Who's covering the clinics next week and how will this impact the endoscopy wait list?" His sidekick wrote everything down. She chewed constantly on gum, always with her mouth open, and occasionally sticking her tongue out with the gum perched at the very end when she recorded some particularly complex matter.

After the meeting, Oliver indicated for me to stay. Climbing right into my personal space and smothering me in the fetid stench of necrosis, he said, "I don't believe for one moment Colin's death was an accident. I've tried to tell you before and I'll tell you now, there's a killer among us. I wouldn't even be surprised if your house fire was connected."

"Colin's death looked pretty clear to me," I said. "In fact, I feel rather guilty because I told him he needed a colonoscopy. I think he was too embarrassed to ask anybody to do the procedure and too stupid to know this could be the outcome. I'm not even sure I could get my finger up my bum let alone a five-foot colonoscope."

"What if I told you that at 7:15 this morning I bumped into Mary

Taylor walking *out* of the hospital as I came in? And I swear she had a bruise on her face. Explain that to me."

"Why don't you ask her? That would be a good start. Or ask the police maybe, but good luck with that when we've already written a death certificate saying Colin had a heart attack and died about two hours later than he really did." I added, not believing Mary could have any link at all, "And you'd, of course, be the next in her sights. I can't imagine she'd want me dead, or Sally White, for that matter. I know she hated Colin. She has since before she even got here. But honestly, Oliver, I think the simplest explanation on this occasion is the correct one."

12

Our First and Last Family Camping Trip

My family and I needed to get away. Money was always tight, but at the moment things were worse than ever. Even before the latest turn of events, Catherine and I never seemed to have enough money for a holiday in a hotel. We considered renting a chalet or caravan but did our sums and instead shelled out on a frame tent. In the long term, we figured we'd save money for more trips in the future.

The camping kit had a large Hessian sack containing metal poles that weighed the same as a small adult. A separate massive bag held the tent. The concept of lightweight poles and fabric was only recently evolving.

We were excited to buy the tent but were immediately concerned as we struggled out of the shop to discover that if we were to go camping the choice would be tent or children, since the only place the kit fitted was across the back seat of the car.

Thus, the cunning plan to save money on camping instead of expensive trips was already faltering. We accepted that the ship had now sailed, and we had to find a solution. This meant buying a trailer. We found one in the "Buy and Sell" pages of the *Kilminster Journal*.

Before I could collect it, I discovered I'd have to get a tow bar fitted. By now, I think we'd spent enough for three weeks in a five-star resort.

I got the trailer from a dubious character on a housing estate on the rough side of town. Unlike the description on the phone, the trailer was about twenty years old and had almost become part of an overgrown garden behind the house.

The owner was an unshaven, dangerous-looking looking fellow wearing a football shirt and dirty grey jogging bottoms. He had a dog that looked to me like a banned breed. It growled and slobbered as it tried to squeeze through the gap in the door to rip me limb from limb. The owner took my cash and closed the door, leaving me to tug the trailer out of the brambles and around to the car. I was surprised there were still wheels on my vehicle by the time I pushed it around.

None of the wiring worked, in part because there were no lights. In my usual way, I lacked the courage to get my money back and chose the safer option of driving home. I was stopped by the police for having no lights and received a fine and three penalty points. The fine was the equivalent of three nights in a Hilton hotel.

When I found a mechanic to replace the wiring, he told me the trailer needed new springs, too. My credit card was full and my current bank account hovered around zero by this point, but we were leaving in a day and I felt keeping this current purchasing disaster to myself was wise.

The trailer was ready by Saturday morning. We planned to leave by ten, though packing the equipment in the car and trailer took longer than anticipated. By the time we had the tent, camping stove, blow-up mattresses, and plastic utensils stowed in the trailer, there was just about room for us to stuff the sleeping bags around the edges and into any gaps.

We were very excited to finally set off on the first of what would be many camping adventures, aiming at a site in the New Forest. Sadly, the weather was predicted to be "unsettled," which of course meant wet.

The weather gradually worsened as we drove south, with visibility down to about fifty yards and the windscreen wipers struggling to perform their task. Our spirits weren't dampened, however, and we listened to Disney tapes the whole way to the campsite. As if ordained by God, the rain stopped and the sun came out, just as we pulled into the site and slowed down at the office to check in. In a movie, there would have been an angelic choir singing as the weather cleared over the campsite.

The kids were beside themselves with excitement and ran off to explore. Meanwhile, I was having my already full credit card swiped by a miserable-looking sixteen-year-old girl with a mauve tracksuit and greasy hair. She didn't actually say much throughout the whole encounter. I believed the sum total of words included *name, card here*, and *take this*.

She grabbed a paper map and drew an *X* on a green area marking our site. Then she gave me a yellow ticket on string to tie to the tent, and we were ready for the adventure to begin.

What I'd failed to notice was that the cover had blown off the trailer and the two remaining sleeping bags were soaked. The others were somewhere between Kilminster and the site.

The rest of the day has been deliberately blurred from my memory and is too financially painful to dredge up. I remember tears, some shouting, a very expensive hotel, a lot of rain, and a visit to a pottery factory where you could paint your own plate. I also recall a family-friendly pub where none of the children ate more than forty percent of their food. My own meal was called Cornish crusted chicken and consisted of some blood-red ligaments and blood vessels with a vague string of meat within from a hen that had died of old age. The crust was a smear of crushed corn-flakes drenched in what looked and tasted like amniotic fluid. I could feel myself adding up the cost of the trip from the time we'd chosen to buy a tent to this point.

We'd parked the car in the hotel lot that evening. Our plan was to try to find an open camping shop the next day to buy new sleeping bags. But after a disappointing buffet breakfast, the tent was gone when we reached the car, stolen from the trailer, though oddly the poles were still there. I'd already concluded that I hated camping and didn't even consider an insurance claim. I just wanted to go home, sell the trailer, and get on with my life. Catherine, however, quite reasonably felt that since the sun had finally come out, we could at least take the children to the beach.

We left the hotel and found the beach. Clearly, the rest of the country had had the same idea. The car park was full, and there were vehicles parked on the verges as far as the eye could see. We drove a good half mile to the end of these cars and found a single car space but not long enough for a car with a trailer.

It was unusual for me to be rash or hasty, but I stopped the car, walked around, unhitched the trailer, and pushed it into a farm gateway. Then I parked in the space and took a screwdriver from the boot to remove my licence plate from the trailer.

Catherine might have noticed I was getting a little agitated about the trip so far. She reassured me that a few hours on the beach would be fun for the children, and I could lay there and read. Catherine even bought them each a fishing net from a little wooden hut at the entrance to the beach — basically, a blue nylon net on a thin bamboo stick presumably made by an urchin in Asia. In one, the net had already split open before we reached the beach.

Catherine believed it would be fun to have a picnic. Or put another way, I felt it would be cheaper than buying food that wasn't eaten and she was trying to keep me calm. I had bought some four-day-old bread rolls, cheese, and sliced ham earlier at a petrol station on the way to the beach.

We found a spot on the sand and laid out the towels to sit on. I finally stretched out on my towel, grabbed a handful of sand, and let it spill out through my fingers. I was left with two cigarette butts in my palm. The wind had whipped up a little, so there was a continuous sensation of being in front of an industrial sand blaster.

In fifteen minutes, the children were bored. The towels we were sitting on were covered in sand. A man ten yards to windward picked up his towel to shake it and a curtain of sand pelted us all in the face. But we doggedly determined to enjoy this adventure and reached for our ham-and-cheese rolls. Predictably, despite being in a separate bag, every mouthful was gritty and removed the enamel from our teeth. I buried mine among the cigarette ends and discovered why I hadn't seen any dog muck on the beach as I did so.

We drove home, sans trailer, sans tent, and not in the least bit refreshed.

13

The Request

The "camping" trip had been a costly few days, so I was excited to see a letter on our welcome mat from a lawyer asking if I'd consider some medico-legal work. I spoke to one of my more commercially minded medical colleagues who told me that this was a potentially lucrative line of work.

"Money for nothing, Brian," he said. Now there was a phrase I'd heard a few times, and it began to hold an appeal.

Writing back to agree, I received a six-inch pile of photocopied medical records a few days later, expecting them to reveal something about a slip on a banana peel in a supermarket. Or maybe a holiday insurance claim by a patient for a thrombosis after a long journey in which the data would be presented and the judge would rule that this was just bad luck. What I didn't anticipate was the patient records of someone accusing one of my colleagues of medical negligence.

I felt physically sick. The doctor in question was a leading academic in London who had been president of our society, had published seventy papers, and was also a self-promoting conceited rat. He was a man who already despised me for questioning his arrogant stance on tainted blood, something that allowed no room for debate. For the first half of the previous decade, he'd strongly denied that factor VIII represented a meaningful risk. I recalled him arguing in a hotel lobby at a national meeting with a Scottish colleague trying to persuade England and Wales to work toward an independent supply.

Moreover, as I read through the case, it was clear that the standard of care fell well below what should be expected, partly because it seemed the patient rarely saw the famous professor and was mainly reviewed by ever-changing junior doctors, seldom supervised, since their leader was presenting at international meetings.

Having read the notes for an hour, I agreed already with the lawyer that the patient had a good case, but I lost sleep that night knowing I was up against a powerful, influential colleague. Was this just my weakness? Or was this how the medical establishment worked?

I wrote my report and sent it back to the patient's lawyer. About two weeks later, I received a response from the professor's lawyer with an aggressive rebuttal. I noticed, however, that there was a paragraph included in his report that had been plagiarized word for word from a journal article and mentioned this in my further response.

That was when things turned nasty, and the justice system was revealed in all its glory.

I was lying in bed reading an Alistair MacLean novel while making mental notes on plot style for *Meat*, my own bestseller. The telephone was ringing downstairs, so I leaped out of bed, assuming it was the hospital or a family emergency. But no, the caller was none other than the London professor with his oily charm and false collegiality.

"My lawyers have told me I should sue you for slander," he oozed. "Your medico-legal report is defamatory."

"I think you mean libel, not slander," I replied, a little shaken but also feeling emboldened by Catherine, now standing in the hall gazing at me questioningly as I hunched there in my winceyette pajamas.

I wasn't entirely convinced that writing a medical report that was true was libel, but there was no way to check on this. My colleague sounded distinctly threatening.

Professor Lowlife added, "My lawyers want me to sue you, but I'm not like that. They told me I could take you for £500,000. But I consider you a friend. If you just withdraw your reports, we can consider the matter over."

"Okay," I said. "Leave it with me."

After a restless night's sleep, I called the lawyer who had appointed me and described the phone call. Within a very short time, the case was settled out of court to the clear satisfaction of the patient. However, after one traumatic medico-legal case, I decided this wasn't money for nothing and wasn't the pool that I chose to swim in ever again.

14

A Period of Calm at Last

Life gradually returned to normal at Kilminster Hospital in 1999. The mode of Colin's death was, not unexpectedly, a source of great amusement for many of his colleagues who were able to switch on expressions of earnestness and sensitivity when required, while in private their gallows humour helped them survive.

But life moved on, and the irreplaceable was always replaced. About four months later, Colin was substituted with Susan Lawless, another enthusiastic new gastroenterologist, who suspiciously lacked any of the normal flaws inherent in this specialty. She was selected by Derek Newby for purely financial reasons, since she wasn't planning to set up a private practice.

I began to question my own stereotype rubric that was able to fit most doctors and specialties into a quadrant based on native intelligence and the level of arrogance they demonstrated. To show this, I created a graph, "Classifying Medical Specialists." I've never published it and it isn't confirmed by academic research, but it feels likely to be accurate.

Surprisingly, it appears that hematologists represent the pinnacle of intelligence and modesty. Who would have guessed? I believed we were actually close to David Attenborough and in the oppositive quadrant from most members of the royal family.

Mary Taylor remained on extended stress leave for four months or so and then one day she was back. Although I never heard anybody raise the same thoughts as Oliver Michaels, there was definitely a cloud over Mary, and I figured one or two others also suspected her in the death of her senior colleague. However, I never heard anybody actually voice this.

When I saw her in the corridor, I approached her, intending to ask how she was feeling. But she fixed me with a gaze that made my sphincters almost fail, so I lost courage and merely nodded a friendly acknowledgement. My house repairs were underway and the last thing I needed was for her to burn it down again.

Our insurance claim hadn't been settled yet, so I finally had to extend our mortgage to get the work started. Catherine urged me to launch a small private practice, but the thought of entitled upper-middle-class patients with mild iron-deficiency anemia secondary to heavy periods filled me with foreboding. Instead, I told her I'd rewrite my book, *Meat*, which was clearly destined to spend several months on the fiction top ten list once it was completed.

H

The hospital clinic was relatively painless on Tuesday. The only vague confusion of the morning was due to a new patient who was referred owing to a low platelet count but denied all knowledge of ever having had a blood test and was certain she was seeing me to discuss the moist fungal rash under her breasts. The woman was a little disgruntled when I told her that was outside my scope of experience, and even more so when I pointed out we still needed to work out what was wrong with her blood. In the end, I pretending to know what I was looking at and elected to avoid eating cottage cheese henceforth.

I finished at the clinic and was walking to my office holding fifteen sets of very thick medical records. My office door wasn't completely closed, so I turned around and backed in. If I'd walked into the office forward, I would have automatically reached to my left and found the switch without looking. But I'd reversed in, and normally in that situation, I'd use the corner of the bottom set of notes to push against the light switch to turn it on. I immediately noticed that the light switch was missing and all that remained was a red and a black wire poking out. The electricians had been doing a bit of rewiring on our floor and not only didn't finish the work but had left the wires dangerously exposed.

I called Jeremiah Foch, but he was off at a very important managers' meeting (VIMM), so his sidekick promised to deal with the light switch immediately. In fact, two sidekicks arrived an hour later, wrote furiously on their clipboards, and had an important discussion about whether this came out of the hematology or general budgets. They were unclear if there were forms to complete and sign, and whether the director of finance needed to authorize the work. Sidekick number two then wisely spotted that we might need to call the health and safety coordinator, and the repair was put on hold.

In the end, it came out of the general interior repairs budget, subsection electrical, and had to have board approval to be signed off. Thus, it was twenty-five days before a new switch was installed.

Agenda: Medical Staff Meeting, Wednesday, September 1, 1999, 5:00 p.m.

Regrets: Daniel Collins.
Minutes of last meeting.
New medical director.
Reduction in nurse support for outpatient clinics.
Revised junior doctor assessment rubric.
Closure of staff car park.
Equal opportunities training.
IT security training.
Annual leave rules.
Any other business.

The medical staff meeting was moved to Wednesday because Monday was a holiday. It took place in a small room at the end of the pediatric ward, which was originally established as a family waiting room. We'd adopted this room, with the signed approval of Jeremiah Foch and the director of finance, to the irritation of the pediatricians. It didn't have a table, so we all had to sit in a circle, most of us on comfortable living-room-style chairs, but latecomers had to find whatever they could to sit on. The last four to arrive sat on twelve-inch-high toddler chairs made of red plastic. The consultants' dining room was now part of the expanding management suite, and each manager's sidekick now had his or her own sidekick to triplicate any note-taking.

"Brian, are you actually listening?" Jeremiah asked querulously.

It seemed Patrick O'Donnell, the new medical director, was asking me a question. He was being introduced to us at this meeting. Richard Headley had considered the role but decided the honorarium barely covered ten percent of his potential loss in private work if he took on the role. The new director could apparently, so it was rumoured, count a pile of fallen matches in five seconds. As it turned out, he was the only applicant for the role, and I'd had four calls from his previous colleagues strongly urging me at all costs not to let him be appointed.

Since this wasn't a decision in which I had any influence, and since the only wishes of the doctors on the appointment committee were one, no interference with their private practice, and two, no risk of increased National Health Service work, needless to say, O'Donnell was unanimously approved.

The new medical director was asking if I'd lead a working group on the use of the outpatient space. As one of the longer-established consultants, I had acquired a look of gravitas and taken on some of these roles, since they all offered a chance of merit awards that might help pay off my constant debt at home. But this was a poisoned chalice I didn't want to accept, so I declined with huge regret and mumbled something about regional hematology commitments. I was slurping my coffee at the time, and as sometimes happened, I performed the process in the wrong order, somehow tilting the mug to sip it when it was only halfway to my mouth, hence pouring it down my front.

Nigel Robinson wanted funding again. I recall something about a new ear syringe. Before he spoke, he extracted some sort of white plastic tube with a decongestant and shoved it up his nose, inhaling deeply in each nostril. Then he made his pitch. "When in doubt, suck it out," he said, both eyebrows raised three times in succession. And perfectly on cue, he added, "As the actress said to the bishop."

It must nearly be time to leave, I thought. My mind generally wandered as soon as Nigel opened his mouth.

I'd arranged for my pager to go off by six to get out sooner, and my ever-loyal secretary indeed phoned at the appointed time. Walking out to the wall-mounted phone in the foyer, I picked up the receiver and heard her insist in the usual comedic conversation whenever called upon to perform this role, "Dr Standish? It's Whipsnade Zoo. We have a chimpanzee with a low white count, can you help?"

As I replaced the receiver, I glanced at my pager and realized its days were numbered because we'd just bought a new mobile phone, though I was reluctant to spend money using the device. Getting the phone had been a very brief negotiation with Catherine, who had noticed that several of our friends had mobiles.

"I think this is essential for your safety when you go to meetings away from here," she'd told me.

"Yes, but I've managed to travel without one so far, and here I am."

"Oh, so you don't care about my safety, either? What if *I* break down on the A67?"

I shrugged in resignation. "Let's go and buy one." Of course, we did, and so began the world after cellphones that was never, in my opinion, quite as fun as before.

H

I already mentioned I wasn't fond of looking back at my school years with any ridiculous yearning for the past. No retrospective reinterpretation was needed. But when I received a letter in the post from my old school announcing that twenty-, thirty-, and forty-year reunions would take place in June, I hesitated briefly enough for Catherine to insist I go.

Today was the day for the reunion. It started with a welcome from the headmaster, who was some new great hope for the school. The previous headmaster had been there for thirty-two years and had recently announced his urgent retirement and immigration to Spain ahead of the publication of an article expected in the *Sun* tabloid. The school governors report made sure to tell us the new head was an Oxford graduate, which presumably made him better than other applicants.

From there, we headed to the cricket field for a match between the old boys and the first eleven. Strangely, I wasn't asked to play, so I looked around for some daisies or a crippled terrier for old time's sake.

I noticed the conversations around me were limited to current jobs, marital statuses, number of children, and subtle estimates of current wealth. We could have saved time with name badges declaring this core dataset.

The first person I recognized in the distance was a fellow called Hugo Smyth whose family came from money a few generations back. Something to do with sugar plantations and a history that no longer seemed anything to be quite so proud of, though the money continued to roll in. Hugo had been the only boy in our class brought to school by a chauffeur. I changed direction to avoid him and immediately spied Marcus Lacy. That prompted a recollection of a biology lesson on fetal development in which we were asked to open our books to page seventy-two where there was a picture of an embryo. Marcus bellowed, "It looks like Brian. Let's call him embryo. Wait! No! Let's call him gay embryo. Gembryo." Marcus's only insult was to call a guy gay. Try as he might, the new nickname never really took off. But clearly it was wasting some of my own memory space for me to dredge it up.

Sitting by the cricket pavilion was Oscar Needham, who did great things at school: rugby captain, always in the top tenth percentile academically. I wandered over to talk to him, not sure why since I'd had no interest in him at school and still had none. As I was about to open my mouth, there was a roar. "Gembryo!" And Marcus came lurching toward us — two hundred and fifty pounds of total bonehead.

In a moment of clarity, I understood that I had only vaguely liked three people at school, and it was very doubtful I'd enjoy them any more now than I had then, particularly as a nascent misanthropic seed planted at this very school was now fully flourishing.

Clearly, I shouldn't have gone to the reunion, especially on a long weekend with Monday off. With an indistinct mumbled "I'm just heading to the loo," I strolled purposefully to my car and set off for home. I'd spent one hour and twenty minutes there that I would never get back.

Heading home, I realized that long weekends used to be for family. This latest long weekend would be a little lonely, since none of my kids were home — the youngest was staying with her best friend and the others were at their granny's, Catherine's mother. As I drove back from the reunion, I reflected on how decades were passing in a flash. So, I made a mental list, as was my custom:

- Riding lessons, ballet classes, football matches.
- Swimming lessons and finding that one inflatable armband was always missing.
- Brownies and Cubs.
- Plastic ball pools, rope ladders, urine, and spit … a chance to expose the kids to a few germs to boost their immune systems.
- The tooth fairy, Father Christmas, Dr. Seuss, and first days at school.
- Birthday parties where one kid never joined in and hung around with the adults.
- Trips to the in-laws, trips home, stopping every twenty minutes for one of the kids to pee and always finding that a shoe had fallen out somewhere along the way back.
- Singing songs in the car or listening to one of the Harry Potter books.
- "I Spy" and "How long will it be till we get there?"
- School projects that somehow needed dried macaroni.
- No prizes on prize day except for the sunshine prize for being a good citizen.

- Head lice, vomiting bugs.
- Peanut butter sandwiches with no crusts trodden into the carpet, spilt orange juice, not eating vegetables.
- *The Little Mermaid*, crying, laughing, *Jungle Book*, bath time, *Snow White*, long cuddles, *The Gruffalo*, bedtime.
- Board games, learning to ride a bike, camping, getting a rabbit, losing the rabbit.

And as the years went on, the list continued:

- Sighing teenagers who didn't really want to go to Nana's.
- More homework, tears over a B minus, the first crop top, skateboards, a lost gym kit.
- School trips, fallout with best friends, first period, first loves, first breakups, sleepovers, parties with secret cider, first vomit from alcohol.
- First jobs, driving lessons, smashed phones, sulks.
- The death of a grandparent, the death of a pet.

And then in the blink of an eye:

- University, dropping them off at the coach station, the joy of every weekend visit.
- The constant anxiety about where they were, what they were eating, who they were sleeping with, and how much (of our) money they were spending.
- Their first loan.

And that was having children. Over so fast, except for the one who dropped out in the second year and became a permanent free lodger creating disproportionate messes and complaining there was no yoghurt or orange juice in the fridge or that a favourite T-shirt hadn't been washed yet.

BRIAN'S SIXTH RULE

You can find joy in your career, your family your hobby, or something else, but you can't have more than three. Choose carefully.

15

The Pregnancy

In October 1999, I was in the doghouse again. Our friends, Tracy and Jeff Lancaster, had recently had a daughter, and I found their parenting method a challenge to our relationship with them. While fully embracing individuality, I felt I was being pushed to agree with some unusual theories and hoped to avoid a Friday evening dinner in favour of blobbing in front of the TV. Indeed, from conception, I'd endured too many details. Of course, Catherine was irritated at my reluctance to go to their house. Even when Tracy was pregnant, we were included in the process very early. I was surprised I wasn't at the conception with a box of tissues and a pregnancy test kit.

Her husband, Jeff, was my accountant, and was pleasant enough. We had a cordial relationship, but rather like a game of Snakes and Ladders, he reached a point where I felt he could be a friend, then played the bagpipes, which was like getting to ninety-eight, throwing a one, and landing on the snake head that took our relationship back to three. Jeff was one of those totally English men who somehow think that because their great-great-great-grandfather had sex with a Scottish peasant in a smoky hut in a settlement in the Highlands, he was also Scottish himself. Suffice to say, he wore a kilt at balls.

Tracy was Australian, but not in the tough outback sense. She was self-diagnosing pelvic instability even at three weeks and was almost fetishistic about preparing her perineum for the birth of her first child. When she was at seven weeks of pregnancy, to avoid stretch marks, tears, and a lifetime of incontinence, she assiduously applied a range of products to her vulva, including but not limited to:

- Coconut oil.
- Olive oil.

- Cocoa butter.
- Shea butter.
- Massage oil.
- Tabasco.
- Butter.
- Spreadable butter.
- Peanut oil.
- Peanut butter.
- Vaseline.
- Marmite (she had preferred Vegemite but couldn't find any in the local supermarket).
- Cherry juice.

Personally, I believe the word *vulva* should never be uttered in the presence of a male, particularly if it was included in a shopping list.

Jeff seemed resigned already to a lifetime of misery, though he looked well fed. All of this was shared frankly with Catherine and me and thus reduced my dietary choices considerably.

By fourteen weeks, Tracy constantly clutched her lower abdomen as if to support the baby, currently smaller than a walnut. She was constantly exhausted and began to eat for two, misunderstanding that this didn't mean for two rugby players. Jeff did his best to cater to her culinary demands but never quite satisfied her.

At twenty weeks, she made a playlist for her delivery. The birth plan ran to three pages and included a paddling pool at home in the living room. Jeff was to be the videographer and serve peaches for energy and ice chips for hydration.

Tracy didn't want to go to the hospital and declined induction or analgesia. Lights were to be dimmed so as not to dazzle the baby, who was to be called Fisher, which had a sad, potentially prophetic irony.

By now, Jeff was in charge of all household duties when he got home from a ten-hour day. He could do no right. Tracy languished on her bed or sofa issuing commands like the captain of a ship. Then she arranged for a doula whose previous job was battering fish at the Silver Cod, a woman who had two kids called River and Moonbeam and who wore a flowing tie-dyed kaftan and vegan shoes.

By twenty-four weeks, there was no space in the garage, which now looked like a high-end baby store packed with boxes and unnecessary but cleverly marketed equipment, including a warmer for baby wipes and a neonatal abacus with music playing a subliminal alphabet.

Every night, Tracy tested Jeff on learning baby sign language, and the fetus was enrolled in a private school.

Thirty weeks coincided with me going to see Jeff to discuss my taxes. By this stage, he was a broken man sleeping in the spare room, since Tracey had put on sixty-five pounds and was too uncomfortable to have anybody in bed with her.

She had turned into an unbearable scold and called the family doctor and obstetrician sixty-seven times. The doula and medical team seemed to offer opposing advice on every issue.

"Bring on delivery day," Jeff told me one day with genuine weariness.

I didn't have the heart to tell him that raising a child might also occasionally lead to marital tension and that perhaps he needed to set a target date twenty-four years ahead.

At forty weeks, there was no sign of Fisher emerging. When forty-one weeks arrived, Jeff suggested curry and sex might bring on labour and received a black eye. At forty-two weeks, Tracy suddenly and unexpectedly became quite calm and almost likable. The doula visited at forty-three weeks and set up some essential oils and whale music. Remarkably, this had no effect. The paddling pool had taken up the whole of the living room for six weeks, and the water had begun to go green.

When forty-three and a half weeks were reached, Tracy called the hospital, and Jeff nervously thumbed through the birth plan. They drove in for an assessment and were offered an induction, which Tracy eagerly accepted.

Thirty minutes later, she was requesting gas and air. By an hour, she was begging for an epidural. Jeff tossed the birth plan into the trash bin.

After another three hours, the baby arrived — a successful normal delivery. Two feces had preceded the baby by forty-five seconds on the floor, which Jeff trod in, later wiping them on the side of the magazine rack in the waiting room.

The baby was named Jane.

I called Jeff with an old joke. Question: "How soon after a birth can you have sex?" Answer: "A gentleman waits until the placenta is out."

He didn't laugh. But he did invite me to stand at the foot of Loch Tay three weeks hence to hear him play a lament on the bagpipes to celebrate the arrival of his first-born. I told him I'd rather put my hand in a food processor.

When my taxes were completed, Jeff called me in to sign a couple of returns. On that occasion, he commented on my poor financial planning and suggested that some of the money I inherited from my father could be invested in a property that I could rent out. I promised to reflect on that.

After we completed our business, he asked, "Did you ever meet Alisha Sharma, the woman whose job you got?"

"I met her at a couple of meetings, but I didn't really know her."

"It's just that she's disappeared from our life, too. She used to be a friend of me and Tracey. I mean, Tracey and I. And after she resigned, she just cut us off completely. Tracy's worried that it's us because she feels you and Catherine are growing apart from us, too, ever since we had Jane."

I struggled not to comment on his poor grammar and sentence construction. Instead, I unconvincingly insisted that we remained loyal and keen friends and said, "Let's go out for some food soon." Of course, that really meant "I have no intention of going out for dinner or even a cup of coffee with you."

I did feel that Alisha had taken her retreat from medicine a little too far, but if I could find her, maybe I could let her know that Tracy was concerned about her.

H

I was going up to London the following day for a meeting at the College of Physicians and was able to walk up a couple of floors afterward to the registration department where I asked about Dr. Sharma. The people there confirmed that a couple of years earlier Alisha had written to state she wasn't renewing her medical registration. The only address the department had for her was a rented apartment in Kilminster.

When my train pulled into the station on my way home, I decided to drive over to the apartment and double-check that Dr. Sharma wasn't still living there. My intention was to ask her to give Tracey a call.

The apartment was on the second floor of a small four-storey unit near the centre of town, just behind the cathedral. It seemed to me as if each floor had either three or four flats. I rang the bell for apartment 304 and waited with no response.

The entrance door was on an electronic lock. I hung around for ten minutes or so, imagining a little spy fieldcraft allowing me inside if somebody exited, but realized that could be a long wait and there was no guarantee I'd be let in even if another resident came by. It was dark and raining lightly.

I looked across from the apartment building where I was sheltering under the porch and could have sworn a man in a car was watching me, but then the vehicle pulled away. Or was that Dr. Sharma? It was hard to say, since I didn't get a really good look. Was she avoiding me? I turned to leave, and as I did, noticed there were fourteen mailboxes, each with a name written in mismatched slips of paper behind clear plastic frames. But it was the name Dr. A. Sharma that stood out for me. So, she really was there and one way or another we were going to talk.

I needed to return. At the very least, she might be able to help me plan a life outside medicine.

16

Investment Plans

On Tuesday, November 16, 1999, Nigel Robinson was standing in the hospital foyer. There was a ten-foot circle of onion fug making this a no-go zone for everyone other than a poor old man in a wheelchair. He was wearing a blue hospital gown open at the back showing his age spots and a scar from a chest drain. His catheter bag emerged from underneath an orange hospital blanket and was almost bursting with dark urine. It appeared the old chap had been parked there and forgotten, the final insult being trapped in the noxious gases emanating from Nigel's armpits.

I turned around, not ready for a game of innuendo bingo, and unable to correct my breathing so that I exhaled as Nigel approached. When he spotted me, he hurried after me. I truly think at that point I would have chosen a below-knee amputation over spending my lunch living in a Carry On film.

He never caught up with me because I rounded the corner and took a sharp turn into the outpatient suite where Richard Headley had just finished his clinic and was leaning on the wall with his right hand, trapping a poor auxiliary nurse who looked as if she fully understood his peno-frontal behaviour but was unsure how to extricate herself.

"Heather, can I borrow you for a moment?" I asked, allowing her to duck under his arm.

She shot me a very relieved look and squeezed out, leaving Headley and his uncontrollable libido appearing somewhat confused.

Heather Webster was usually with me in my hematology clinics and was a perfect oasis of kindness supporting my patients. She was also perfect for Richard. Two X chromosomes and aged less than fifty — he cast a wide net.

Her sister was the librarian in our hospital, which predictably fascinated Headley. "You know what they say about librarians?" he asked me.

"No, I don't think I do."

"They're like nuns. They go like trains."

"Is that so? Like *chuffa-chuffa-chuf*? Or more like *woo-wooo*?" I asked, my voice laced with sarcasm.

He stared at me, unimpressed.

I was unclear what sort of sample size was needed to gain statistical significance for his assertion, but even for Richard, I felt it was perhaps at best unproven and wondered if a research proposal would get through the Ethics Committee. These colleagues of mine were the front line of medical care, a truly frightening thought.

The afternoon outpatient clinic usually started at 1:00 p.m. and finished around 4:45. Halfway through, I sent a patient for an ankle X-ray, expecting him back fairly quickly. I asked Heather to search for him, and she returned about forty-five minutes later with Terry Saunders, one of the radiologists, who asked to see me between patients. It turned out that my patient had misheard the name being called in the waiting room and had taken the appointment of another patient.

Sadly, he ended up having a barium enema. Terry thought he was going to be sued. I felt it was unlikely that a patient who attended for an ankle X-ray and ended up with a tube up his backside with contrast medium being poured in would feel brave enough to confess this to a lawyer.

The reality was that most patients didn't sue their doctors, and when they did, it was the one least expected to complain. So, Terry and I elected to go with a heartfelt apology, and everyone was happy, including the patient who had been diagnosed with colonic polyps that could now be sorted.

The barium enema incident reminded me of how unpredictable the average human being could be. I started thinking again about the hemophilia HIV situation and questioning a system that failed patients at so many levels, followed by attempts at high-level coverups.

Medicine was about randomness at infinite levels. There was probably a complex formula to express this.

When we attended medical school, we were taught anatomy and normal human functions. We were told what could go wrong such as infection, trauma, cancer, or autoimmunity. And we were informed about the treatment. Simple. Diagnose according to the criteria, then prescribe the solution.

We were even given an hour's lecture on how to communicate with patients, with ten minutes at the end on breaking bad news. But what weren't we told? They didn't tell us there were seventy-two different types of patients of differing age, sex, and size, and that one size fitted all was a myth. And that, as a result, patients behaved in seventy-two different ways.

Most diagnoses bore only a vague resemblance to the textbooks. And the evidence for treatments was often zero, or worse, manipulated by Big Pharma with the assistance of financially conflicted colleagues who were happy to be paid six-figure sums each year to travel around telling everybody why one treatment was the best. Or that hospitals were in a constant state of controlled, or uncontrolled, chaos, and that in the history of management degrees, nobody ever chose to be a hospital manager.

Another thing we were never told was that the Ministry of Health was run by politicians advised by dysfunctional humans promoted to a level of incompetence who provided non-evidence-based advice with a healthy core of financial consideration underpinning the reports. And who cared only about the next election, not the health-care workforce ten years ahead.

Lab tests weren't always reliable. They didn't tell us that some patients faced anxiety at work or domestic abuse. But the other things they didn't reveal were that nurses could bully one another, managers were all desperate to demonstrate the right data had been collected, and many psychopaths or sociopaths had the perfect personalities to rise to the top in competitive fields of medicine. Also, that sometimes the correct thing to do wasn't what was said in a guideline because that applied to a mythical perfect average patient.

The textbooks also didn't tell us there were so many variables, including the patients, their wishes, their diseases, the tests, the availability of treatments, the wait times to see health-care professionals, and the knowledge and style of the people seen.

Of the numerous individuals involved in this random soup, everyone had their own anxieties about children or money, or sick relatives or what jobs they really wanted to be doing. And despite human subjectivity, amazingly, patients mainly did well.

Artificial intelligence hadn't yet taken our place, but sometimes I wondered if it might be more reliable. Or would we still get a patient lying on a radiography table speculating on how pouring all that stuff up his backside helped to image the ankle?

My brother had remained very well, and I was somehow using him as a metaphor for my patients. There was a regular adjustment of his medications chiefly to find something with tolerable side effects. He'd finally told Mum and seemed disappointed that she already knew he was gay, since he was pretty sure she'd seen him as a bachelor playboy.

Mum rarely left her house now. She'd developed severe low-back and rib pain and didn't feel safe to drive. My mother tried to make her usual jokes, but they now came from a place of sadness, and while we still laughed, we all knew it was part of an elaborate dance around the truth — she was dying. On the other hand, Harvey pointed out that plenty of people got back pain and that my constant obsession with death and dying wasn't at all helpful. His perspective was that she seemed unchanged and that the back pain had occurred as a result of working in the garden.

H

On Wednesday, the seventeenth of November, my next patient was in the outpatient clinic room. She came in with her husband and wanted me to look at her right big toe, which she thought might be infected. The woman crossed her right leg over her left and pulled off her sock. By a miracle of physics, somehow the sock caught her ingrown toenail, which was hanging on by a thread, and catapulted it across the table straight into my mouth. While I was spitting it out and trying to clean my tongue with alcoholic hand sanitizer, the patient stared at her husband and said, "Who are you?"

"Um, I might have entered the wrong room," he answered, appearing a little uncomfortable. He had mysteriously thought he'd heard his name called, and upon seeing his mistake, had been too anxious to get up and leave. As I said, medicine was full of random events.

I finished the clinic finally and arranged to have lunch with Bobby Norwich, our rheumatologist. We headed to the main canteen and searched for a corner table, since staff and patients' families were now intermingled and we had to be far more cautious when discussing cases. When we sat down to eat, he told me about Sharon, one of his patients, who he'd seen that morning with a swollen knee.

"Young people with swollen joints sometimes have chlamydia, a sexually transmitted disease," he informed me a trifle unnecessarily. "Sharon's twenty and I asked her if she'd had any new sexual partners in the past three weeks."

What follows was the conversation Bobby had with Sharon as relayed to me.

"Actually, yes," she said, concerning her recent past sexual partners.

"We may need to test him, too, if you're positive," Bobby told her.

"There's more than one."

"That's okay. We can arrange two separate visits."

"There's more than two."

"How many are we talking about?"

"Sixteen."

"In three weeks?"

"No, sixteen in one night."

Bobby said she seemed pretty proud of this achievement. "So just how did this happen?"

"My friend and I had a bet about who could have the most shags in one night, and some army recruits had similar ambitions."

Chlamydia had definitely won that particular evolutionary race, but Sharon came a close second.

After lunch, I had an administration afternoon, a chance to run through a few results and complete a couple of junior doctor evaluations. I wanted to chase Dr. Sharma again. For some nagging reason, I had a ridiculous notion there was something wrong. I called medical staffing and was able to get the phone number for Alisha Sharma's apartment. When I dialled the number, there was no disconnection message. But my call wasn't answered and didn't go to an answering service. I phoned Maureen Potts, a friend of Catherine who worked in medical staffing and persuaded her to check Dr. Sharma's file. She told me that my predecessor was single and there was no next of kin defined in her file. But beyond that, there was no other information she was prepared to reveal.

So, I tried a different approach. Dr. Sharma's apartment had a management company, and I called its number and found myself speaking to a young woman who seemed quite pleasant despite her Scottish accent. I told the woman I was Dr. Sharma's cousin and was anxious about her, since she hadn't been in contact. I also told her Alisha had diabetes and sometimes lost consciousness, which was enough to coax out some information. She assured me that Alisha was alive and well and had specifically insisted that if people called asking about her, they were to be told not to try to find her. Alisha had informed the management company that she no longer worked as a doctor and didn't wish to reconnect with anybody.

Dr. Sharma was up to date on her rent, and yes, somebody had recently been into her flat to check the gas appliances, and everything in the place was normal. My brief spell as an amateur detective came to a reluctant end, and I accepted that Alisha had probably escaped from her career at a good time. Perhaps I should draw inspiration from her move.

That got me thinking about the advice to find a house to rent, and when I was home, I reached for the free local paper to look at the real-estate listings. And there it was: a large old Victorian on the edge of town within our budget and already adapted into three apartments. Catherine and I excitedly left a phone message with the estate agents with the aim of visiting the house on the weekend.

On Saturday, when we saw the home, we were very pleased. The property we'd found in the paper seemed perfect for our investment plans. We could put down thirty percent and get a mortgage. By our calculations, we'd make more than enough to cover the repayments and then create a nest egg for ourselves. Money for nothing.

It was a huge redbrick Victorian building. The neighbourhood wasn't entirely perfect. The next driveway along on the right had a Vauxhall Chevette on bricks as well as a white van that had previously belonged to British Gas but had the letters peeled off. The neighbour was just coming out of his house, so I gave him a wide neighbourly grin. I wasn't sure he really saw me, because his face was more of a scowl than a smile. He had interesting teeth, though, that would have challenged any dentist. From where I was standing, they seemed to have feathers stuck to them, and I wondered if he'd just eaten a baby bird. Then I decided he appeared quite horrifically intimidating and quickly glanced away, pretending to admire the guttering on our proposed purchase.

On the left side, the driveway lacked a little love and would have been at home in the Serengeti. It, too, boasted an old car, this time a Nissan Bluebird on bricks. *Our* house, because I'd already decided it was perfect, had a front lawn converted into one large parking area. There were no cars there today, but there was an old washing machine. We were let in by the estate agent, a six-foot-two man who might have been thirteen years old and who wore a grey suit that would have fitted somebody five inches shorter, with a grubby white shirt he'd somehow buttoned up incorrectly so that the buttons ran out when he got to the collar. The fellow had tried to hide this with a shiny navy blue nylon tie. He was trying to grow a moustache, unsuccessfully, and had the annoying swagger of a Cockney street trader but without the authentic accent.

The man ushered us through the front door, and we walked straight on into the first flat. The whole main floor had been converted into a potentially beautiful one-bedroom apartment with a kitchen, bedroom, and large living room, which looked out onto the shared pebble driveway. It smelled a little damp with an additional aroma of vegetable soup mixed with urine. I noticed that as we first passed through the front door that there was a rather ugly second door at the foot of the stairs leading either straight into the main floor, or upstairs to another door that led to the largest apartment.

The large upstairs flat had four bedrooms, two of which were small attic rooms on the top floor. The teenage estate agent took us upstairs to proudly show us the avocado bathroom suite with gold taps, which had several years' worth of toothpaste and spit on them. The toilet appeared unflushed, but apparently it was iron in the water causing the unpleasant staining.

Every bedroom door had about three Yale locks, each put on by, I imagined, a drunken student with no tools. Catherine and I toured the rather downbeat dated rooms undeterred and returned to the ground floor to view the last flat.

On the left side of the house, there was a concrete pathway to the back garden, and halfway along, there were steps leading to a basement that had been converted into what was described as a studio apartment, essentially a kitchen, living room, and bedroom in one large space in addition to a small bathroom about four by five feet, consisting of a toilet, sink, and shower. The ceiling was mildewed, and I was fairly sure there were slug trails on the damp carpet.

Nevertheless, I fell in love with the house. Catherine was also carried away by her imagination of glorious rooms she'd seen in *Good Housekeeping* magazine: dappled morning sunlight shining through wooden venetian blinds, croissants, freshly squeezed orange juice, a red-and-white-checked tablecloth on an old oaken farmhouse table, perhaps a throw, whatever that was. She excitedly discussed options all the way home and insisted we put in an offer immediately. Best to do it today in case the estate agent had secondary school on Monday.

We could see past the smell, the damp, the dated kitchens and didn't pause to consider the potential cost of renovations. All we could think about was the glory and wisdom of our decision to become property developers and landlords.

17

The Death of Kevin

There was a general air of agitation over the impending meltdown of all IT systems at the stroke of midnight on New Year's Eve, which dominated the staff meeting.

Agenda: Medical Staff Meeting, Monday, December 6, 1999, 5:00 p.m.

Regrets: Daniel Collins.
Minutes of last meeting.
Year 2000 virus precautions.
Nephrologist interviews.
New junior doctor feedback process.
New educational method training. Outcome-based learning. Mandatory training.
New rules on ink colour for charts. Sign the register that you have acknowledged these.
Reduction in study leave allowance.
Annual leave rules.
Any other business.

Other agenda items were compressed into a few minutes after nearly an hour of pointless speculation. Patrick O'Donnell, our new medical director, had suddenly developed an evangelical zeal for banning all colours in medical charts other than black, which I found particularly galling, since I'd spent the last decade of my career writing in a particularly fetching turquoise. He had also reduced our leave for meetings and conferences and had tightened up the annual leave. O'Donnell knew how to keep us onside. He also demanded we all complete further mandatory instruction on how to train our junior doctors, the method for which seemed to change about every eight months.

Nigel Robinson was unhappy if a meeting occurred where he didn't propose something, so he rose to stand as always. I noted the vacant seats either side of his own; colleagues had chosen to stand at the back of the room rather than breathe from the sides of their mouths for an hour.

This month, Nigel advocated for funding for a new clinical skills training program to diagnose atrophic vaginitis in elderly patients. I gagged as he presented the case for training. I didn't do well with anything between the neck and knee. He continued. "I believe they'll want hands-on training … nudge-nudge, wink-wink."

I sighed. Was this to be every meeting for the rest of my career?

It was hard for me to focus on the meeting, since I was in the doghouse once more. We had six hens who shared the attention of Kevin, our cockerel. Kevin, who had the same sexual appetite as my cardiology colleague, Richard Headley, was dead, and it was all apparently my fault.

This was all part of a neighbourhood dispute in danger of escalating. Awkwardly, one of my hospital colleagues with the annoying name of Bunty, a pediatric surgeon, was involved in creating the tension. She owned a large Burmese mountain dog that when it defecated produced two- or three-handers about three pounds in weight each. They looked as if only an elephant could have passed them. Bunty, really her name, glanced around her whenever the dog performed, and if she saw nobody, hastily walked on. I knew this because I'd seen her do that.

In the autumn, Bunty kicked a few leaves over the poop. In the winter, she might flick snow over it if there was any around. The challenge was that a different neighbour was convinced my dog, Stan, was responsible for the offending piles and was incapable of seeing that a canine couldn't produce a greater volume of feces than itself.

I wasn't friendly with the complaining neighbour. I always thought he looked like the sort of person who dressed in leather underwear and watched pornography in his garage. A retired clerk from the local town hall who had spent his whole career in the waste-management department, he had dark oiled hair, a rosacea nose, a pencil moustache, and a mousy timid wife always ten steps behind him when they were out and about. She seemed to be constantly praying, perhaps for her husband's sudden unexpected death.

This neighbour came around over the weekend while we were eating our breakfast. He wasn't wearing leather underwear but was definitely a little excitable and started twittering on about our cockerel crowing in the morning, which in his opinion wasn't very neighbourly. I felt he was being a little ridiculous, considering we were living in the country. Catherine took all this to heart and already felt everyone was watching us to see if we left heaps of dog poo around the place. The next morning at five o'clock, Kevin began to crow.

"You're going to have to go and kill him," Catherine said, nudging me awake. "It's not as if he serves any function."

This felt somewhat extreme but was a measure of how distressed Catherine was feeling about the worsening neighbourly relations and how comfortable she was with the cycle of life.

Obedient as always, I put on my dressing gown, and looking a little like Noël Coward, wandered down to the garden with a fish-landing net and a small hatchet. Kevin was very compliant. He learned of his sentence and made not a sound as it was carried out. I put him in a plastic bag and threw him in the back of the car before going back upstairs and getting into bed. "The deed is done."

"Oh, I feel so guilty," Catherine lied, clearly not enough, having sent me to the garden to execute our beloved baby.

With perfect timing, as her words left her lips, we heard a loud *"Cockle doodle dooooooo"* as a different rooster rose for the day. With a terrible realization, we knew that poor Kevin was innocent. And that was the main reason I was against capital punishment.

H

Our nephrologist, Janan Khan, had retired and we'd advertised the post three times with no interest. Then, finally, we had two applicants and more or less agreed that, however weak, one would be appointed. Thus, her replacement would either be a guy I'd been to medical school with, Chris Abbott, or a new female graduate, Kathy De'ath, from Oxford, who had an excellent CV, four publications in peer-reviewed journals, and strong references.

I was sure Kathy would be the one we appointed and was pleased to be asked to join the interview committee along with Joyce Rush, the director of finance; Richard Headley; and the Reverend Cyril Leahy, our very elderly previous hospital chairman, who seemed to me to not quite understand his role on the panel. The interviews were on Tuesday, and we talked to Chris first.

He'd been a consultant down south but had left after five years. No reason was given, but it was an open secret that he'd had an affair with a colleague's wife. In his previous post, the nephrology service was in total disarray and the national nephrology association had been consulted for advice on how to solve the numerous issues in the dialysis suite. I felt it was unlikely that we now had the man who would fix our own problems. The highlights of the interview went as follows.

"Why are you moving from your current post after such a short time?"

Chris grinned. "Because I hear your renal service is in dire straits and needs me to rescue it."

"What do you like doing when you're not at work?"

Chris grinned again as if knew the job was his. "Anything you can do while holding a gin and tonic."

"What can you bring to this hospital?"

"I have my reputation and a good selection of Côtes du Rhône." Again, I think he thought this was a boys' club, and judging by Headley's smile, my colleague didn't feel that was even remotely an appalling answer.

"Can you give us an example of where you've had to deal with conflict in the workplace?"

"I'd say every day of my life, conflict follows me." Chris chuckled, but none of us cracked a smile. Even Richard could sense this might not be a good answer. If the worst interview ever could have been scripted, this was it. The man was unemployable. He was a vile chauvinist moron who didn't belong in medicine.

When Chris and I were at medical school, he was known as Houdini. He'd perfected the art of arriving late when most of the work was done and disappearing whenever things got busy, yet always passed a rotation with flying colours. Why? Because he asked in-depth questions on ward rounds, having already looked up the answers the day before. I was surprised that he could perform so badly in an interview but was relieved that after this performance he wouldn't be joining us.

Then it was Kathy De'ath's turn to shine. Inevitably, we got off to a bad start when Richard made the obvious joke about her last name and her patient mortality. I honestly thought he believed he was the first to see the potential pun. It was time for Headley's first question. "Ms. De'ath, are you married?"

"No."

"Do you have a boyfriend?"

"No"

"Thank God for that. The last thing we want is you going off and getting yourself pregnant."

I winced when I saw the candidate's face.

"If it helps, I'm not going to have a baby," she replied, features not losing their composure.

Richard smirked at me as if we were in on a good joke, and I sensed the hope of Kilminster Hospital slipping away in front of my eyes.

Kathy stared directly at Headley and continued. "But my partner's currently trying to get pregnant."

"How does a man get pregnant?" asked Cyril Leahy, whom I'd thought was asleep and who maybe wasn't the perfect choice to represent an average patient.

I tried to save the interview, studied my list of questions, and asked, "Why Kilminster rather than an academic career? Your CV shows us you have an interest in research."

Richard should have been posing the clinical questions, but so far had asked none that we'd planned. I'd been delegated to ask the general questions.

"I'd really embrace the challenge of redesigning your service. There are a few ways we can handle the wait times such as changing your dialysis clinic protocols —"

Headley immediately interrupted and countered with "Oh, so you're going to change everything as soon as you arrive?"

I didn't let her answer this, since no good would come of it, but intervened with "What do you like doing when you're not at work?"

"My partner and I enjoy volunteering at food banks. We also like bell ringing."

I smiled at her and felt perhaps she was beginning to feel a little less threatened. "What other skills can you bring to this hospital?"

Before she could answer, Richard said, "Other than ticking our diversity box," which was greeted with silence.

I jumped back in. "Can you give us an example of where you've had to deal with conflict in the workplace?"

"Honestly, I think I can see some current potential sources of conflict, and I'm going to withdraw my application," she answered stiffly, and even Richard stopped grinning inanely as she stared him down. She rose to leave, thanked the interview committee, and in a very dignified manner, left the room.

"What a bitch," murmured Richard.

"How's her husband going to have a baby?" asked Cyril.

"What have we done?' I implored no one in particular.

And so it was that Chris Abbott was appointed to the nephrologist role.

H

Apart from being an appalling colleague, Chris Abbott was what women who should have known better called dangerous. They found him appealing despite the reality they weren't going to be "the one." And as soon as they learned he wasn't the one, they were the first to complain. Most knew what they were getting into, and that included Olivia, my current second-year resident. I was aware of this because on call one weekend they had sex on my desk, leaving behind a crumpled journal and one alarmingly ginger pubic hair.

I'd given Olivia permission to use my office to prepare a case report. They hadn't expected me in that weekend. The sight of Chris's undulating, spotty buttocks scars me to this day.

But I loved it when karma struck.

I was at a regional meeting only two weeks later in another hospital fifty miles away. The gods had ordained that the genitourinary clinic was near the hematology department, so it was with some joy as I headed to the room that I saw Chris emerging from the clinic, and even more joy when he saw me.

Here was a potential ethics dilemma. Your colleague maybe had chlamydia, warts, or some other sexually transmitted disease. Should you tell your junior doctor who either gave it to him or received it from him? Or is that a breach of confidentiality? I thought about all that during the meeting.

Of course, the first image was a bush of ginger pubic hair, which put me right off my rich tea biscuit. I suppressed the terrible picture to the darkest recess of my brain. I figured Olivia knew that I knew, and it wouldn't be unreasonable to suggest a visit to occupational health without mentioning I'd seen her special friend in a genitourinary clinic. Monogamy had a lot to commend it. *If you like your partner. of course*, I thought to myself, with Sally White and Neville returning to my mind.

That got me speculating about Mary Taylor. She wasn't the woman she used to be, and while the woman she used to be left something to be desired, I still felt anxious that perhaps there was something I could do to help her. I vowed I'd talk to her. She'd become isolated. I had no doubt that Oliver Michaels had shared his suspicions with anybody who could stand the cloud of toxins long enough to hear them, and that would have gotten back to her.

H

The following week, there was a drinks party, and Chris was there with his current partner, who hung on his every word. They presented themselves as the perfect couple, other than at one point going in to slightly too much detail — zero was enough — about what they got up to at home with a camcorder and a jar of low-fat mayonnaise. My mind was drawn to medical school slides of warty penises and discharges, and I put down the baked Brie I was about to eat, which led to my eighth rule.

BRIAN'S EIGHTH RULE

When a couple at a dinner party tells you they're having great sex, they're having none.

That rule worked every time. Like all my rules, though, this one required expansion. As such, clearly, it applied to most bragging, money, and children's intelligence.

H

I was now at the phase of life when several colleagues' children were at junior school. There was a sub-clique among the consultants whose kids went to the local independent school. And these champagne socialists whined continually about the school fees, yet never actually removed their children to attend a perfectly acceptable state school. Instead, they leaned on the headmaster to give them bursaries and discounts, and the process of negotiation was akin to buying a rug in a Turkish bazaar. The headmaster had even contacted me and offered a buy-one-get-one-half-price deal on school fees. Somehow the endowments left by some ancient benefactor for the poor of the parish all became grants for the children of the most well-off in the vicinity.

At every party one endlessly heard how exceptionally gifted Cordelia or Rupert were. Traditionally, a few years later, Cordelia and Rupert then

HENRY AVERNS

claimed to have dyslexia because this allowed an extra hour for all examinations and increased the chance of attending the chosen medical school. Indeed, one of the vile progeny, Persephone, had even been given a scribe to do the writing, claiming apraxia — her mother, Cressida, pronounced this *apwaxia*, owing to her upper-class lisp. Persephone had won the music competition early that year playing the violin, grade eight, so I very much doubted that holding a pen presented that great a challenge.

But it was essential for Persephone to get into medical school. For medicine was, indeed, the only acceptable career for these children. It had struck me a few times that these kids who became doctors, who needed the extra time through school and university, might represent a major clinical risk when writing a prescription. But it seemed that the dyslexia faded away at about age twenty-three.

Not so my offspring, who stubbornly hovered on the median or just below, and in whom any sort of employment would be a triumph.

I didn't like parties of any sort. I believed people essentially didn't really want to talk to me, and I definitely had no interest in them. And I was incapable of faking it. When I was a kid, people who drove ambulances were called ambulance drivers. Then one day they suddenly became paramedics. When someone told you they were a paramedic, there was always an almost indiscernible pause when you were legally obliged to be impressed and in awe. It was as if they were some sort of philanthropic war hero. The same thing applied to firefighters. You had to be impressed. You couldn't say, "Don't you get bored watching videos and homoerotically competing in the fire station gym?"

But tell people you were a hematologist and they glazed over. And that was my experience whenever we went anywhere. There was always a bloody paramedic somewhere basking in undeserved glory. Even at meetings of the Association of British Haematologists, or as Catherine called it, the Association of Boring Haematologists, socializing didn't come naturally.

Hospital Christmas parties were the worst of all events. Indeed, one of my huge dreads was the table for ten where six to eight people already sat there. You saw their faces fall as you approached the table, then found an empty table, with no other couples to join you, as if you had cholera. This latter situation was a balance of pleasure because you didn't have to talk to somebody about their children, job, or last vacation, but was also tinged with a vague sense of being untouchable.

Chris ranted about his interview at the Christmas party that year. He'd heard that the other candidate and her partner wanted a child and were planning on sperm donation and in vitro fertilization. Chris smirked that he could find a way to save them £2,000. His current partner had a black eye after sustaining a squash-related injury earlier that day, and she decided to go home at about nine o'clock, so he was free to be as vile as his reputation had predicted.

He then spotted Margaret Crocker and couldn't stop himself from telling her that from the angle he was standing her moustache was the best in the whole room. This was only fifty minutes into the evening, and the event struggled to gain any momentum after that point.

At the moment, when things couldn't get any worse, our host, Fiona, a local GP, tried to raise the level of mirth in the room by recalling the time when … well, actually, let me start at the beginning.

It was a Thursday evening. There was an unexpected knock at the door just as Catherine was cooking supper. I went to the door to see Joe Wordsworth, my colleague from Bristol, with his wife and two children.

"Joey, come on in. Great to see you. What can I get you to drink?"

"Wow, that smells amazing," said his wife, Jane.

"Let's go through to the garden and have a drink," I suggested.

We went into the garden and drank, and Catherine came out and nudged me to go inside for a moment. "God, are they ever going to leave?" she asked me. "You'd think they were here for supper or something."

My blood ran cold for a moment, but I agreed with her.

They left in the end, and we ate a slightly overcooked evening meal and laughed about how inappropriate the Wordsworths had been coming at that time and staying for two hours.

The next morning in clinic, Joe called me. Normally, I wouldn't accept a call when seeing a patient, but the phone rang in the clinic room and I felt I should answer it.

"You forgot to tell Catherine you invited us to dinner, didn't you?" he asked.

I confessed my sin.

The ensuing chain of events showed that this year the fates weren't pleased with me. The patient who had been sitting in the room when I took the call obviously found this very amusing, Ss much so that she told her family doctor, who a few months later invited us to a dinner party and chose to share the story with Catherine, who until that moment had no idea what had happened on that fateful Thursday evening.

We left the party and drove home in silence. I believed I remained in the doghouse that time for at least five days.

It was at this same party that Mark Stone, GP, rugby player, and self-adoring God, suggested to me that we start meeting at the local gym every Sunday. He actually patted my belly as he said that. If I'd been a foot taller, tougher, and slightly more muscular, I might have responded. As it was, I smiled but vowed to go to the loo and not wash my hands, then pass him a canapé later that evening.

"Kilminster Manor has a private gym and squash court, Brian," Mark informed me further. "You look as if some ab exercises wouldn't go amiss."

I'd never heard of an ab, but this sounded like a positive move, so four of us agreed to meet in two days' time.

As we cleaned our teeth that night, Catherine squeezed my biceps muscle. "I must agree with Mark. Your muscles are like a bag of flour."

18

Renovations

In December 1999, on a Saturday, our house purchase was completed. We'd imagined the keys would be ready by nine in the morning, so I took a day off work, hoping to get in and start planning. But it was five in the afternoon when we were given the keys, and dark and drizzling. We still drove over to see our new house, but oddly the electricity had been turned off. So the following morning, we headed back to the edge of town to take another look.

It was raining again, and the skies had that heavy grey oppressive look that could go on for weeks. Our house looked a little less loved than I recalled, and there was a white van parked in our driveway. In fact, I could make out the words BRITISH GAS where the original stickers had been peeled off and knew this was my neighbour's van. We tried to squeeze in next to it, but the washing machine was in the way, and he'd parked right in the middle. Ideally, there should be space for three there.

We parked on the road and let ourselves in. Catherine had decided that standard paint from the do-it-yourself store wasn't appropriate for a grand old Victorian and that we should buy top-end heritage colours. But to give her due, she asked me what colour I felt we should choose. I suggested magnolia.

"Oh, for God's sake! That's the colour of every room in your parents' house."

"What about terracotta?" I suggested.

"No, that won't do. I think we go for either otter brown or svelte sage. Which should we choose for the accent wall?"

"Oh, definitely the otter brown," I replied.

"No, the sage is the right choice."

I nodded. "I totally agree."

Paint colours chosen, I bravely walked around to the neighbour's front door to ask him to move his van. It was dark. I was frightened. I knocked about as lightly as a mouse. There was no response. I rushed back to our driveway, telling Catherine there was nobody home.

On Sunday, we drove back to our new rental property first thing. We were meeting an electrician to repair an issue in the upstairs kitchen that was fusing the lights in the whole house. The white van was still there.

"You really need to go and talk to him," said Catherine.

I knew she was right, but I was conflict-averse and a little reluctant. But with some encouragement from my wife, I walked around and knocked on the neighbour's door. It was about 9:30 by then. There was no answer, so I knocked again, then spotted the bell, which I rang.

When I was just about to walk back, the door opened and the creature I'd seen before stood there in a dirty stained vest and some equally soiled Y fronts. Between the two hung his large white belly like a fatty apron that had hidden his genitals from sight for the past few years.

The creature said something. If I was absolutely honest, I was only able to satisfy myself that this was a Northern Irish accent and that he was almost certainly going to shoot me through the knees. I was a good twenty feet away and unlikely to be chased, and not really knowing what he'd said to me, I asked, "Could you move your van?"

There was an explosion of Viking language, or something akin to it, and then the door was slammed shut. I scurried back and reassured Catherine, who was now inside, that I'd dealt with the problem.

The electrician came, and it was no surprise that the job would be much bigger than we'd anticipated. I asked him for a quote.

"Everyone thinks of changing the world, but no one thinks of changing himself," the man replied.

Nobody likes a cocky electrician.

We spent Sunday afternoon at home. I hadn't looked at my novel *Meat* for a few months, so I dug out my notes. With the benefit of time and reflection, I realized the book was a little weak and set about rewriting: "It was windy. Damn windy. In the distance, a train passed. Charley Steel sat in his laboratory." I'd changed the protagonist's name from Chet to Charley at Catherine's insistence.

"His laboratory assays were underway." Catherine had felt this sentence was a little lame and that perhaps I could comment more on the haunting darkness of the research centre's corridor. I vowed to return to the sentence.

I'd had one of those moments of genius the evening before when Catherine had cooked me salmon pasta with asparagus. When I noted the odour of asparagus in my urine, I recalled that some people couldn't smell it. Or was it that some people didn't make the chemical that smelt? I couldn't quite remember. What I did know was that this represented the perfect point in my book when my hero realizes there's a murderer in the lab stalking him. The killer had to pee and is unaware he's left a scent that will lead to his discovery and downfall. Pure genius.

In the end, though, I had writer's block and put away *Meat* until the artistic juices started flowing again. In any case, I had to get ready to go out.

My new exercise buddies and I had arranged to meet at the gym at seven on Sunday evening. I threw my new gym bag onto the back seat of my Honda Civic and headed to the north side of town just off the ring road. The manor the gym was in was an impressive redbrick mansion with a long drive and a pebble parking area in front of the main doors and reception. I went in, holding my stomach in a little, and spoke to the receptionist, who told me the gym was tucked away from the main building on the east side and that I'd need a card to get through the door.

"Are you a gym member?" she asked me.

"No. This is my first time. But I'm meeting a member."

"I'm afraid you'll have to pay, sir. It's £30 for non-residents and non-members, but you'll have access to everything, including the pool."

Grudgingly, I paid and walked out again, crunching over the gravel to the building in question. I found the back door to the kitchens where the chef, who looked as if he had three weeks of food smeared on his clothes, was smoking a cigarette.

I asked him where the gym was, and he said something in a thick regional accent that sounded a little threatening, so I backtracked to reception where I was given instructions to make my way around the east, not the west side of the main building. Thus, I was the last to arrive.

The gym was tiny — a small room stinking of rubber mats and sweaty bodies. It had a pull-up bar, some weights, an exercise bike, a treadmill, and a large grey ball about two feet high. Through some fogged-up glass, I could see the pool, which unlike the photo at reception, where it appeared to be fifty feet long, was actually about twenty feet and ominously cloudy.

Mark was already there on the bike, nine miles in. There was a pool of sweat below him. His skin shone slick with perspiration, and he made worryingly sexual-sounding grunts. Tim was running on the treadmill like a gazelle, as if he could do thirty miles without breaking stride. I hadn't broken into a run since 1976, though I'd once done a sort of run-walk for a train and staggered breathless through the door, only to discover the train wasn't leaving for another ten minutes. Meanwhile, Warwick Tetlow appeared to be pushing the wall in one of those odd warm-up displays experienced gym enthusiasts were supposed to engage in.

I was sure my body was incapable of exercise and abhorred the feeling of raising my heart rate too much. So, I elected to use the weights, grabbing the second from the right, figuring that reaching for the five-pound ones was a little wimpy. My plan was to begin with ten pounds and work up. Before I moved over to one of the mats, I was certain something tore in my shoulder. "Forty curls!" yelled Mark, looking around and flicking a cupful of sweat that landed on my face and arm.

Managing half a curl, I pulled my bicep and abandoned the weights, deciding to lie on the grey ball. I'd seen my wife doing this at Pilates and was a little disappointed that I couldn't even find a position of stability or balance.

I rolled around on the ball, gazing upward until I thought I might vomit, feeling slightly absurd and consuming zero calories. Then Mark offered the bike to me. I scrutinized the moist shiny saddle, had an alarming visual image of sweaty genitals, and claimed a new knee injury. Hurrying off to the change rooms, I stood facing a corner as I slipped out of my gym kit, hoping that my rather overweight pasty body wouldn't be seen by the other three. It was a sad situation, since I'd been into town the day before to buy some running shoes, shorts, and a sporty-looking top saying NIKE. It hugged my abdomen alarmingly, even at extra large.

Mark had needed a shower and now stood in the centre of the change room with his penis dangling like a donkey's, chatting away as if still at the dinner party. Try as I could, I kept finding my eyes drawn to the horrific sight that looked as if it could rupture a uterus.

"I've got to get home, sorry, chaps," I said.

Just before I left, Mark produced a small plastic bottle of talc and liberally applied it to his shaven genitals. The sight of that white phallus haunted the rest of my evening.

"Not going to stop for a pint?" I heard from three testosterone-laden voices as I dashed to my car, vowing never to return.

I did confess to Catherine that I was unsure if this was a good fit, and she thankfully told me she didn't like too many muscles in a man. That put me in a strong position.

19

Year 2K

New Year's Eve was creeping up fast. Not much would happen between Christmas and New Year's, and I was able to get ten days off.

There had been frantic management activity for several weeks because the predicted computer meltdown at the stroke of midnight as the new year started, known as the Y2K bug, was supposedly going to destroy our hospital records system.

Our head of IT, Alan Gaylord, was out of his depth. He'd been appointed in 1984 on the basis of having bought one of the first Amstrad computers. Alan was pretty competent at using a handheld calculator but was incompetent at everything else, including communication with human beings. He strutted about like a peacock using computer words such as *hard drive* or *RAM*, but most of us could see through the charade.

His crowning achievement was when he programmed the system to identify inappropriate or potentially offensive words utilized in searches, assuming users were searching for pornography sites. These included basic anatomical descriptions such as *breast* and led the system to send warnings to the IT department whenever perfectly reasonable words were employed. His system became known as "Alan's Lexicon of Porn," and inevitably the list was circulated, much to his displeasure.

Alan had muddled along in the role fairly well until hospital IT systems actually became the underpinning foundation to practice, at which point, like IT managers across the country, he'd appointed a team of two competent technicians who had carried him ever since. Inexplicably, he rose to the challenge of Y2K as the final face-saving solution, issuing memo after memo and a range of protocols that were remarkably identical to an article in *What Computer* magazine's November issue. Most of us could barely raise the enthusiasm to care, and some, such as Richard Headley, positively prayed for an IT crisis just to raise the level of excitement for a week or so.

Catherine and I had arranged a fireworks display in our back garden to welcome in the new century. I created a playlist of cleverly curated songs about the year 2000 or the new year, while Catherine made some party snacks, and we invited all our friends along. Both of them, I should say. In addition, we invited the neighbours, believing them to have planned a trip to Tenerife. To our dismay, they hadn't, and they accepted the invitation.

There was nothing specifically to dislike about them, but I preferred it when they were next door to when they were in my house. They were a little too cheerful. The husband, Trevor, owned a shop in town selling books specifically related to Tudor England. It was fairly niche and wasn't doing as well as his wife, Penelope, had predicted. Meanwhile, Penelope was a suspiciously cheerful Christian who was simply too smiley and happy to be trustworthy. My preference was to look for the worst in my fellow humans. In her version of the world, everybody was wonderful. She even liked me.

Penelope had cornered Owen Keegan, a friend who had been unemployed for as long as anyone could remember and spent his wife's earnings with abandon. She was inviting him to attend her church, unaware he wasn't currently searching for God.

Owen had bought a "Year 2000" firework for £500, which would rise up and actually display the figure *2000* in red lights before gently drifting across the sky. Owen had been rattling on about this for a month and getting increasingly excited to launch it. I'd spent £40 myself on four rockets, which I had let off far too early in the evening before it was properly dark, so I was feeling the pain of wasted money.

Tessa, Owen's wife, ran a pre-school childcare facility surrounded by other people's hideous children whom presumably she had to pretend to like. At least it put her in a perfect position to care for her husband, who behaved most of the time like a three-year-old, other than when he had a credit card.

The evening might have been better if we'd started at eleven. However, we'd invited our guests for six, and it was clear within thirty minutes that the night was going to be tough. Owen told Trevor that all history was boring, but the Tudor variety was top of the list of wasted time. Trevor sulked for the rest of the night. Penelope was overbearingly excited for the new millennium and could only see a wonderful future. The CD I'd burned skipped and clicked and then got stuck on Abba singing "Happy New Year" over and over again.

Catherine suggested we play a game. I wanted to go to bed. Penelope smiled away and talked about the reward she got from volunteering. Owen found a bottle of Scotch given to me by a patient and was quickly two-thirds of the way through it. Trevor disappeared, going home to get an early night's sleep.

All bad things end eventually, even failed dinner parties. I managed to sort out the CD, and Prince was now singing something about 1999. We trooped outside to watch Owen's firework announce the new millennium, timing this to perfection and lighting the fuse at five seconds to midnight. It released a desultory fizzle, like the sound of a hot frying pan being dunked in water. Then it glowed red on the grass for about five minutes, leaving dead turf that didn't recover for four months. A prophetic start to the new century.

As we gazed at the path of burnt lawn, a terrible wailing of bagpipes arose from somewhere on the street. I wasn't sure what I hated most about bagpipes. Maybe the sound, or perhaps the fact that people who played them believed everybody else enjoyed the racket. Either way, I grimaced, and we moved indoors to find Owen vomiting into the top of my baby grand piano.

I called my mother to wish her a Happy New Year. There was no answer. So, in a state of high anxiety, and guilt that I'd once again been the worst child, I called Harvey, who told me that in the past few weeks she'd been feeling much better and had decided to go away for four weeks to Portugal with a recently widowed man from the Rotary Club whom she'd originally met up with, clearly somewhat prematurely, to discuss euthanasia. I found it hard to get the unpleasant thought of my mother copulating in the Algarve out of my mind.

Going back to work after the break felt like stepping onto the gallows. To say the least, I wouldn't describe myself as full of enthusiasm for the year 2000.

20

Cardiac Arrest

I drew a lot of 3D arrows and criss-cross shapes as the latest medical staff meeting droned on. Nigel Robinson was to present to the League of Friends an introduction to a new funding target. He was planning to discuss something to do with elderly care — incontinence or falls. I couldn't recall which. He asked the chair if he should remain seated. "Or would you prefer me erect?" he added, one eyebrow rising. He really did need a bullet. This month's agenda seemed unusually long.

Agenda: Medical Staff Meeting, Monday, January 10, 2000, 5:00 p.m.

Regrets: Daniel Collins.
Minutes of last meeting.
Review of outpatient space.
New method of giving trainee feedback. Pendleton rules.
Remediation of failing students. New policy.
Training in new IT system. Remember no training means no access.
Introduction to 360-degree feedback for consultants.
New rules on pharma food sponsorship.
Annual leave rules.
Any other business.

The improvements to the Clinical Education Centre, to be funded entirely by the pharmaceutical industries' donations, was discussed. We were to have a new lecture hall and two new clinical teaching rooms. The building work had already started. The chair then moved on to request that to avoid conflict of interest we no longer allow pharmaceutical representatives to support meetings with sandwiches.

My new plan was to use these meetings to rewrite *Meat*. I had transferred the laboratory to Istanbul, which had the mystique and atmosphere I wished to capture. Once again, Charley Steel was in his lab, sweating through the night, since there was no air conditioning: "It was hot, Damn hot. In the distance, an owl hooted. Charley Steel rose from his chair, his thigh muscles bulging as he headed for the washroom."

Already I could imagine Catherine disapproving this short paragraph. She would feel it was too sexual. I crossed out the word *thigh* and tried to think of a way to make Charley seem invincible. I could see the potential for the book to be a series. Once the novel was published and in the top ten fiction list for a few months, I could plan my retirement and perhaps write one book per year. I then pondered whether there were owls in Istanbul. I wasn't sure. Maybe a camel? I needed to look at a map and see where Istanbul was.

Meanwhile, the meeting lumbered on. I couldn't concentrate because I was in the doghouse. Catherine felt I wasn't assertive enough. We were refitting the rental house kitchen and there was a delay getting some sort of hinge that allowed you to get your tins and pans into the corner. The contractors said they'd be back when it was available but that the worktop couldn't proceed until the corner cupboard was complete. They installed a bit of plywood worktop as a temporary measure, but we were now five weeks further in, and to my surprise this was my fault.

"Call them, Brian," Catherine told me. "Tell them this is unacceptable."

"I did call three days ago. Why don't *you* call them?" Those last five words were said silently, of course.

"You're so unassertive."

I did as I was told and called them. The hinges weren't in yet, they informed me. That was my fault, of course.

With the white van continuing to park in our rental house, Catherine remained unimpressed by my cowardice. I pointed out that I'd asked a lawyer — actually, a patient who was a lawyer — who told me this wasn't a criminal matter and could be tough to resolve. He'd said that the best course of action was to talk to the neighbour, but I had resisted since I was fairly certain the man belonged to some paramilitary group, judging by his demeanour and accent.

At least we'd managed to rent the basement and the smaller apartment. The large one, surprisingly, wasn't proving popular. No takers at all so far. That concerned me because we'd put at least another £15,000 into the building, not to mention countless hours of painting.

🄷

On Tuesday, I needed to get up to the fifth floor to review an in-patient. I spotted a nurse and a porter pushing a patient on a bed heading from the admitting ward to coronary care. They were just getting into one of the elevators. Regardless of my waist size, and the advantage of using the stairs, I decided there would be space if I squished in on the left side of the bed. No sooner had the doors closed and the elevator started its infinitely slow ascent than the patient's ECG, on some equipment at the end of the bed, showed he'd gone into ventricular fibrillation.

The nurse and the porter glanced at me. I stared at them. The dead patient looked at none of us.

"He's in VF. We'd better shock him," said the registered nurse, who exuded authority, experience, and confidence. I was truly flattered that she considered I might have any knowledge at all and foolishly nodded in complete agreement.

It had been many years since I'd touched a defibrillator. The nurse was already producing some gel pads to put on the chest wall. That was new. In my day, you squirted some blue gel on the chest. I held down my panic.

I grabbed the defibrillator paddles, and the nurse inquired, "Two hundred joules?"

I agreed, of course. The defibrillator let out a high-pitched tone. *Well, here goes*, I thought as I firmly pressed the paddles to the patient's chest and punched the red buttons.

I'd seen enough television medical dramas to remember the "Stand Back" command. However, I was in a tight spot in an elevator, leaning over a metal cot side with my groin pressed against it.

Two hundred joules produced enough current to put the patient back into sinus rhythm, fry the nerve to my left ring and little fingers, and reveal to me an ample insight into the torture technique of several despotic regimes.

I was undoubtedly, metaphorically, and literally shocked. But I swore the porter and nurse gazed at me with new admiration at resuscitating a patient. As the doors opened, I expected an adoring crowd cheering me, but the throng wasn't there. Still, I felt the least I should do was accompany the patient to the coronary care unit.

Once there, the patient was transferred to another bed, and I grabbed the notes to record what had occurred, excluding the fried genital part. I glanced up at the patient's monitor, which revealed a rhythm I knew wasn't normal and could see the patient lying as if dead. I leaped up, grabbed the paddles again like a professional, and gave him another two hundred joules, this time standing back. He rose from the bed, possibly two feet into the air, as he shouted, "Fuckin' 'ell!"

Four things happened then all within a few seconds. I noticed the leads weren't yet connected to the patient and were bundled up on a chair by his bed. The patient opened his eyes, understood what had happened, and thanked me for saving his life not once but twice. The patient's wife approached the bed and also thanked me.

Headley looked from me to the chair and back to me with a massive grin. "And that's why you're not a cardiologist. You can leave this with me now, Brian."

And to Richard's credit not another mention of this was made, and the following day a Harrod's Hamper was delivered to my office with a note from the patient's wife: "Dear Dr. Standish, thanks for saving my husband."

The first Scottish oatcake in the hamper was mildly flavoured with guilt, but I reconciled myself to the fact that the patient had actually arrested in the elevator, so really there wasn't a massive difference when analyzing the facts. I could be a politician with that sort of logic. This was a good introduction to my third rule.

BRIAN'S THIRD RULE

It's lower than you think.

That rule worked for most things in life, but essentially it was a command to be aware of the anatomy of any situation and to extend that it implied not to engage in a procedure without knowing what you were doing. Or more specifically, to work within your competence. It was close, of course, to my second rule, which was to be humble enough to tell the patient you weren't sure.

BRIAN'S SECOND RULE

Embrace the phrase "I don't know."

I'd been evolving these rules over a few years, having struggled to landmark some of my own procedures. But it took about ten years of practice before I felt comfortable saying I didn't know the answer.

That crystallized when our son's Aylesbury duck Daniel became unwell with worms. My wife had pointed this out and caught Daniel, who had a long tapeworm hanging from his behind. Not one to handle any creature, I ran off to grab some yellow marigold washing-up gloves and a pair of tweezers.

"I'll try and pull it out," I said, raising the tweezers and trying to catch the worm. I tugged. "Wow, it's really hanging on. I'll pull a little harder." The worm must have had some sort of teeth to cling to the duck's rectum, but in the end, I gave up and called the vet, who insisted she'd never heard of a duck with worms. "I'm here for another thirty minutes if you can get Daniel down here now."

We raced to the vet's. When we got there, she took Daniel into the treatment room and we waited patiently, along with a woman with a whining Jack Russell in a cardboard box, which was trying to escape. Every so often his head appeared from the top of the box, and his mistress lazily slammed her leg down on its head and told him to lie down.

The vet emerged with a well-practised grim expression, which said to me, "Daniel has worms and you need to give him this potion, which will cost you £80, along with £120 for me seeing him and telling you."

What she actually said was: "We need to amputate Daniel's penis. I don't know what you did to it, but it's basically dead tissue, as if you stretched it for the past two hours."

It was an interesting situation to make a decision to subject your duck — value approximately £10 — to a £200 procedure, because you'd spent two hours tugging on his penis with a pair of tweezers. We agreed and paid the money.

Daniel died three days later when a mink killed all of our chickens and ducks. But at least that helped define my third rule: to practise within your competence.

Sadly, these examples represented the reality of procedural medicine in the 1980s and 1990s, and probably before and after.

On call for internal medicine, I remembered the dread of having a patient who needed a temporary pacemaker or other invasive procedure, because the medical culture at the time meant you didn't consult a senior colleague. So up and down the land, junior doctors carried out procedures based on the "see one, do one" principle of education, which was often "read about one, do one."

When I looked back now, the argument that this was the best way to learn seemed weak. Patients surely wouldn't consent to these procedures if they really knew the truth. I wondered if this was rather like a hemophilia patient consenting to being given factor VIII in the 1980s. Would they have accepted if the true risk had been communicated? Were doctors well placed to make this judgment?

H

Friday was a dark day. It had started off fine. Headley had invited me to his three-monthly cardiopulmonary resuscitation teaching with a group of junior doctors who seemed as if they were about to start secondary school. He had a lifelike doll in front of him called Beryl, or something like that. She had no legs, a rather pouting mouth, and looked like something purchased in a darker part of Soho.

Demonstrating the five breaths, Richard leaned over the dummy and blew. I swore he used his tongue. He somehow made it appear more like a Casanova movie. I had a terrible insight into what the female part of an actual coupling would experience with Richard. Then he passed me a tiny alcohol wipe, a little square of white paper about one inch across with which I was meant to wipe his spittle off Beryl's lips before I performed the respiratory component of the CPR. I became hugely self-conscious and was quite reluctant to do it when I was literally saved by the bell, for Headley's pager sounded, hailing us to a cardiac arrest in the Fleming Wing.

In a hospital with more than its fair share of tragedy, a further death had occurred. It was Barb Tomlinson, the pathology receptionist. She had choked on the sort of chocolate delight that would have been presented at an embassy ball: large, round, and covered in flaky nuts. But exactly the size of her trachea, apparently. The chocolates had been left in my office, a gift from a patient. Since I was on another diet, I'd donated them to the pathology administration team.

I wasn't there at the time, but the death was supposedly rapid. The staff had clearly waded through four or five chocolates already when Barb had popped one into her mouth. She had started to choke, and her colleague, Estelle, had slapped her on the back a few times before noticing Barb was turning distinctly blue. Estelle had attempted a Heimlich manoeuvre, but it was unsuccessful, so she had rushed off up the corridor toward my office screaming for help.

By the time my secretary, Dorothy, had returned, Barb was as dead as a dead thing can be. They had called the cardiac arrest team, which rather ironically resulted in Headley and me arriving before it, since I was with him when the page went out. He didn't run. That didn't suit his image.

He laughed, not in the least perturbed that a soul was leaving this planet. "The juniors will have this sorted by the time we get there." Instead of running, he performed a brisk walk, with me racing along beside him like a toddler shopping with his dad.

The cardiac arrest team took ten minutes to show up because none of us knew the pathology department where I currently worked used to be called the Fleming Wing, and so the various on-call doctors and nurses dashed around the hospital searching for it. In fact, Headley and I were there second and third, the only person before us being the ECG technician, who already had the corpse connected to her machine. And as always, despite the fact that it was self-evidently a lost cause, CPR was started, but no air could get into Barb's lungs because of the large chocolate.

By now, we had three managers present, too. Headley seemed quite neutral about the whole episode, with a look of someone who had casually wandered down to see what all the fuss was about. I noticed him standing about twenty feet away merely observing before turning to leave and giving me what I was sure was a meaningful expression, which sent a shiver through me.

A postmortem the following Tuesday morning confirmed the death by chocolate, which coincidentally was the name of the cake Catherine had made on the weekend, which now seemed less appealing.

Annoyingly, since Barb was dead, there was nobody around to process the postmortem paperwork, which sat there for several days until some quite justified complaints from the family to the management were voiced.

Her body was released the following week.

21

A Couple's Trip

I spent most of our June meeting subtly texting my brother, Harvey, who had agreed to help me with the British Gas van man. He said he'd go over and talk to him that evening. Meanwhile, we had another lengthy agenda to plod through.

Agenda: Medical Staff Meeting, Wednesday, June 14, 2000, 5:00 p.m.

Regrets: Daniel Collins.
Minutes of last meeting.
Review of out-patient space.
Staff carpooling proposal.
Reduction in mileage allowance.
IT security training.
Annual leave rules.
Any other business.

The hospital car park seemed to me to be the only thing making any money. There was no longer a dedicated staff car park and anybody who arrived any later than about seven in the morning was lucky to find a space. The nurses parked on local streets because the daily parking fee represented their first hour of work. This was having a knock-on effect with the locals who complained they couldn't park in front of their own houses.

Jeremiah Foch's sidekick, in a rare moment of initiative at one of our meetings, came up with the ridiculous notion that we should carpool. Aside from the fact that none of us lived anywhere near one another, she'd failed to factor in that most of us wouldn't choose one another's company, and also that we all started at different times.

That led to some lively debate during which Richard Headley described the consultant staff as lions led by donkeys, at which point the sidekick grabbed her clipboard and flounced out of the room.

That night, Harvey was waiting for me in the kitchen when I got home, a smile on his face.

"All sorted, Brian."

"You actually spoke to the terrorist?" I questioned, amazed.

"He's not even Irish! He's from Estonia. And he seemed perfectly pleasant to me. You won't be seeing that van again or even the fellow."

That seemed to me a rather too-perfect outcome. I knew Harvey well enough not to dig too deeply. It always came out in the end.

Catherine shot me a look that was a little too smug and clearly aimed to transmit telepathically that a real man would have dealt with the situation a long time ago. "Can you fix the tenants now, Harvey?" she asked. "Nobody's paid any rent for three months."

Sadly, Catherine was correct.

The tenants had all proven to be terrible choices. The woman in the basement flat told us she'd developed something that none of the specialists she saw was able to diagnose or understand. Apparently, it meant she couldn't work, but luckily, she'd been able to secure a range of benefits, and an electric wheelchair that wouldn't fit through the door and was currently still at the shop. She suggested I should pay to install a ramp and a thirty-six-inch door. The woman had crutches for getting around at present, which even to my eye seemed more of a burden, since she walked around holding them up.

Other than the day we'd met, when she'd seemed totally normal and well, I'd never seen her wearing anything except pajamas, which always had a smear of tea and gravy down the front. When challenged about the lack of rent, she told me quite openly she had no intention of paying and that if we tried to evict her, we'd be breaking some sort of landlord and tenant act I'd never heard of. We hadn't even bothered to get her to sign a contract, since she'd seemed so sweet when we'd first met her. I found myself having thoughts now that surprised me, all of them culminating in her demise.

In the ground-floor apartment, there was a middle-aged couple, the Smiths, who had changed the locks immediately upon their arrival and whom I hadn't set eyes on from the moment they'd moved in. I had no idea what they did for a living, since I'd never asked. But looking at Mr.

Smith, I'd bet he was a history teacher in a girls' school, with his slightly long, grubby hair, glasses, beard, and a vague stink of onions. These were the days when beards weren't so commonly seen and were a useful aid to spotting a deviant.

"Corduroy jackets are the badges of inadequate humans," my father used to pronounce, always oblivious to the absurdity of his sweeping statements, though they did have the annoying habit of turning out to be totally correct.

Once again, with the Smiths, I'd made the deal on trust without a contract. They drove an old Austin Allegro with a Greenpeace sticker on the back window, and a distinct odour of vegetarian lasagne wafted under their doorway at any time of the day.

In the upstairs apartment, we had somehow ended up with one person in a space fit for five or six. While we'd been away for a few days, Harvey had tried to help and invited a man to rent it on the understanding he had four friends who would join him. Those friends didn't exist.

The following week, our new tenant's face was splashed all over the *Kilminster Journal* as a convicted sex offender now being charged with violating the conditions of his parole. At least this raised the odds of getting him out, but judging by the smell of cigarettes permeating the apartment, I suspected it would need repainting to hide the stench. I was a little anxious about how it would be left and decided that since I didn't wish to touch anything in there, I'd have to spend more money on professional cleaners.

By Thursday, the rental house had taken over my life and I was getting increasingly stressed. At this stage, I was deeply regretting ever imagining I was cut out to be a landlord. I was imagining outcomes for all three sets of tenants that would allow us to vacate the building and sell it at the first opportunity. Money was now only flowing in one direction.

To make matters worse, the tenant with the mystery illness told us she was certain there were rats or squirrels in the house. Could I deal with that immediately? And when I did so, could I please not wear any perfumed products, since she told us she'd recently been informed by her doctor that she had a serous allergy to all chemical scents.

I sent Harvey to investigate, spraying some Old Spice the kids had given me for Christmas on his sweater. With luck, she'd mysteriously perish as he entered the property. I knew, however, that if the so-called scent allergy that so many high-maintenance patients complained of were true, then there would be piles of bodies at the entrance of every department store in Kilminster.

Clearly, I needed a property management agency.

Harvey called me later that evening and told me she was correct. There was definitely a vermin infestation. He also mentioned he'd sprayed himself with Brut aftershave, oblivious to the Old Spice on his sweater, and that the tenant hadn't even sneezed.

Infestation? Even the word stressed me. To save money, Harvey told me, we could try to deal with the problem together rather than have pest control people do it. Certainly, I had to slow down the cash I was pouring into the building.

Irritable, I went to the do-it-yourself store to buy more stuff for the rental. To make matters worse, some parents had left their children to roam the shop. I spotted an uncontrolled child with bright ginger hair cutting in front of my shopping cart. So, I made an indiscernible but effective move to the right, blocking its path and jamming it against the spray paint shelves, resulting in a number of cans falling to the floor.

As the child burst into tears, I carried on as if unaware of what had just happened, feeling ever so slightly less stressed. Perhaps that was the answer: maim a few annoying, uncontrolled kids.

I bought the list of products Harvey had requested.

On Friday, I took day off, planning to go to Hereford for the weekend. The vermin could wait a few more days. We were just getting into the car when Harvey, who somehow seemed to spend more time living in our house than his own, told me there was a phone call for me from Public Health about the infestation. Could I meet one of their officers there today? Catherine was angry. This was my fault, of course. We agreed to pack the car for the trip and meet the officer together, then get on our way.

The meeting was actually not too painful. We all concurred there was something dead in the wall, and Catherine and I were forced to admit there were clear signs of "vermin entry" through a cracked drain cover. But thankfully, a fine wasn't imposed, just a ticket, explaining we had fourteen days to rectify the problem. Luckily, the officer's mother was one of my patients, so I think he believed if he didn't meet me halfway, I might withdraw her therapy.

We then set off for Hereford in a somewhat sombre mood, but Catherine was determined we were going to have a fun few days away and put on her tape of Kenny Rogers's greatest hits. That was all it took to get this cool couple rockin'.

My wife and I had been on holiday with couples five times. All five of those couples had now separated or divorced. So compelling was our curse, that we no longer went away with other families.

We'd met the first couple, Sky and Geoff, on a trip to northern Wales. Their names should have been a warning to us. We hit it off so well that we agreed to meet again the following year and rented a cottage. Before we'd been in it for five minutes, their wild son, who was four, had hung on the towel rack in the bathroom and pulled it off. Sky insisted on changing her baby on the green velour sofa and managed to get poop all over the cushion, which she scrubbed clean with the cloth we'd just used to clean the kitchen, taking the colour out of the cushion.

A year later, Geoff was clearly tiring of Sky. She was now an evangelical vegan and perseverating about her latest grievance at work against a white male colleague who had had the temerity to complain she dried her reusable sanitary towels on the radiator behind her desk.

"That's disgusting," I said.

Sky concurred, misunderstanding me completely. Geoff just stared at me, a silence that said everything there was to say.

Did all of this make me prudish … yes, somewhat. Behind the times … definitely. Sexist … no not at all. I disliked most people equally regardless of sex, gender, colour, and religion.

I blamed my mother, though since Harvey was opposite to me in almost every way, that might not be fair. My mother never used the word *breast*. We always had chest of chicken. She never allowed my dad to squirt windscreen washer when it was dirty. I never understood that until my Aunt Jean, who proudly got gonorrhea aged forty-six, told me it was because it reminded her of an ejaculation. Consequently, we ended up stopping regularly for my dad to clean the windscreen when filling up.

One holiday in northern Wales, in a static caravan in the rain, Harvey asked if we could go to the site shop and spend the money Granny had given us. We came back with two T-shirts, printed on-site. Harvey's showed a nut and a bolt holding hands as they ran. One of them read LET'S GET SCREWED. Mine had the logo I'M A MOUNTAIN MAN, I LOVE MOUNTIN' WOMEN.

Neither of had the faintest idea why our mother was so angry, but she marched us back to the shop, had a sotto voice but clearly angry chat with the owner, and replaced the T-shirts with one with she approved. We spent the rest of the summer each with the same T-shirt, which had a picture matching the logo SAVE A TREE, EAT BEAVER.

Despite all of these warnings, Catherine and I agreed to go on a holiday with a friend of my wife's, Alison Goldstein, and her husband, David. They both seemed rather dour. Alison had a look as if she'd just eaten a dried prune and discovered it was cat feces. She'd somehow managed to find a collection of dresses, all of which would have been high fashion in a 1960s maternity shop. Alison clearly had a penchant for white frills around the neck of everything. David simply appeared depressed. To be fair, I could understand that.

They had two children, Candida and Melena, which I felt were particularly cruel names. Alison had been close friends with Karen Morgan, my colleague who had died in the car crash, and was struggling to come to terms with losing her. She was also friends with Mary Taylor, who had changed considerably since returning to work, and who was now separated from her husband.

I tried to imagine two more miserable-looking women than Alison and Mary. Their coffee mornings must have been a riot.

With the Goldsteins, we rented a house in Hereford. The children were staying with Aunt Jean. Our plan was to visit a few National Trust houses. The first evening, I made sausages and ham with mashed potatoes, my speciality. At no point had Catherine told me the Goldsteins were Jews. How was I to know? They both graciously agreed to eat the mashed potatoes, but Catherine was distinctly frosty with me for the rest of the evening.

The following day, I arranged a circular walk around a National Trust garden, ending up at a pub in Canon Bridge, following the footpath to the village. I had bought an ordnance survey map of the area and had planned the route a few days earlier but had left the map at home. Nonetheless, I remembered the location of the bridleway and footpath and led the way. At the first stile, I climbed over and walked on only to hear Catherine muttering that I hadn't helped her and how could I be so ungallant. She glanced at Alison, who clearly agreed, and I felt the chill of two women communicating telepathically.

Alison lagged behind, complaining that her open-toed sandals were getting muddy. The skies were heavy with rain, with that ominous sense one had just before the first fat drop hit the face. It was now or never. If we climbed the gate to our left and proceeded straight up the field, at the top, we'd see the pub and cut half a mile off the hike. Catherine expressed doubt; Alison was merely dejected.

"Are you sure you know where you're going?" asked Catherine.

We reached another stile. I climbed it and stood on the other side with my hand ready to help Catherine over. Studiously, she ignored my hand and muttered that she wasn't sixty yet. This was a good example of the Standish Enigma: "it's best to accept that this exists, but it will never be understood."

David scuffed his new waxed jacket on the gatepost and started desperately spitting on his finger and rubbing the vague mark as I marched ahead with a confidence I didn't feel but keen to be first to the top of the field to allow me quickly to adjust our direction if necessary.

As I reached the crest, to my dismay, I saw no village, no pub. I did, however, spot eighteen frisky bullocks that spied me at the same time. They began as one to trot toward me, then broke into a full gallop. I turned on my heels and ran. The others watched, initially confused, then bolted in fear for their lives. I was the first over the gate by twenty yards, followed by David.

Alison had stepped in cow dung and was clearly livid. Catherine simply made whooping farm girl noises that had the bizarre effect of making the bullocks stop running and start grazing. The secondary effect was to make me seem a little like a gutless deserter.

I suspected this would be a story Catherine would embellish and repeat for years to come. In the end, we went back to the rented house to allow Alison to wipe the cow dung off her toes. Then we drove to the pub. I decided to get the first round, and to get the rather morose couple a little livelier, I chose a local craft beer. Alison expressed her disapproval, saying David always became belligerent if he drank alcohol at lunchtime. David didn't reply, but I caught him casting her a look that conveyed his thoughts on her comment.

We had a rather quiet drive back to our accommodation. It was only two in the afternoon and had started to rain.

Catherine asked what we should do for the rest of the day. I was going to suggest perhaps slowly removing one another's toenails might be fun, or maybe working our way through the obituary column of the local paper. David suggested Scrabble. Alison had brought a 4,000-piece jigsaw puzzle with a picture of York Minster. Catherine thought both would be frightfully fun. Frightfully? I asked her later when she'd ever used that word before.

In the end, I decided to go for a walk alone in the rain. To my dismay, David decided to join me. We made it to the Red Lion. He had four pints of beer and ordered pork scratchings. He smiled. "Don't tell Alison." We played cards, had a wonderful afternoon, and wandered home at six to a happy pair of wives who had almost completed the whole edge of the puzzle.

For four months, we thought we'd finally broken the curse, but sadly the Goldsteins separated three months later, and at that point, we vowed to end our couples retreats permanently.

We were beginning to ask ourselves why we were the exception, enjoying each other's company. Catherine was a woman of infinite patience. She was also possessed of a unique quality — she hadn't ditched me. I'd never been the ditcher in a relationship, only the ditchee. And that included the full spectrum of brush-offs from initial polite rejections through to well-planned desertions.

Not being able to help myself, I composed another list:

Ways I've Been Ditched

- Clare Spooner: *I'm ditching you.* Total hours spent with her — one.
- Joanne Flower: *It's not going anywhere.* Twenty minutes into the first date.
- Helen Gardener: *I'm not attracted to you. It's not going to work.* That was when I called for a date. I'd even tried kissing the mirror to see how appealing I looked. The answer wasn't very, and I had to clean off the smudge with a sock.
- Mary White: She simply didn't turn up for a date. On the way home, I saw about forty people having a party in her house.
- Yolande Holmes: *We've grown apart.* I'd seen her once for a coffee.
- Dianna Lowe: *I'm going to university in Japan.* She was actually working in lingerie in Marks & Spencer.

Additional reasons to avoid me included:

- I'm a lesbian.
- It's not you.

- I need some time alone.
- I need to find out who I really am.
- I'm confused.

Thus, when Catherine became the first woman to agree to a second date, I knew this was the fabled blue moon.

22

Fractured

On a Monday in July 2000, I was in the doghouse once more. My wife had a tibia-and-fibula fracture at the left ankle and somehow it was my fault. It had happened a couple of days earlier. I had just mixed a wheelbarrow full of concrete to put in a gatepost when I saw her head at the window. "Brian, can you come in and help me for a moment?"

"Can it wait twenty minutes? I'm just about to pour this concrete.

"Oh, okay then."

Thirty minutes later, I went into the house to find her lying on the sofa a little pale and sweaty. "I think I've broken my ankle."

She'd been making pâté and had just stepped out of the shower when she remembered it was time to get the concoction out of the oven. The pâté was being cooked in a pan of boiling water. As she got it out, she slopped boiling water onto her bare foot, since she was only wrapped in a towel. She dropped the pan, the water and pâté crashed to the floor, and she slipped and somehow kicked the oven door as she fell.

Being a hematologist, I had no clue if it was broken. "It's probably a sprain," I said, poking at the leg and eliciting screams and whimpers. "We'll give it another hour, then decide what to do." I really didn't relish a trip to Emergency to linger in a waiting room for three hours.

An hour later, she was still lying there moaning pathetically with her bruised ankle, so I drove her up to the door of Emergency and suggested she hop in and I'd call back in an hour to see how things were going. I knew she was going to be sitting there all evening.

About forty minutes after that, she called me. "When are you coming back?"

"Well, I've just started to descale the coffee machine and it has eighteen minutes left. It will probably take about half an hour or so."

"Oh, okay."

When I got to the hospital, the consultant, a colleague, was looking at her X-rays, which revealed a displaced fracture that was going to need internal fixation. But all I could hear at that point was Catherine asking, "How's the coffee machine running?" She had an expression that spoke of days of servitude ahead to allow me out of the doghouse.

Her mood was already tense because her brother, Ian, a vet in Cornwall, had called the previous Friday in a state of high distress. My understanding was that a woman had brought her eight-year-old spaniel in to have its anal glands emptied and nails cut.

"Do you want to be there with him?" he'd asked the woman.

"Absolutely not. I'll pop in and get a video from Blockbuster. We're looking forward to a quiet evening at home with a bottle of wine and a film. I'll pop back and pick up Rusty in thirty minutes."

Ian thought this was an odd response but recognized that everyone had different ways to cope with loss. Subsequently, he euthanized Rusty, having picked up the wrong chart, and the ensuing events were too traumatic to be mentioned further.

Suffice to say, the woman's video-and-wine plan fell by the wayside, and Catherine had insisted Ian come and stay with us until the dust had settled back in Cornwall. Personally, I suspected he might lose his vet licence and rather dreaded him coming, because at his happiest he was a morose man. The broken ankle seemed an excellent reason to cancel his trip, so on balance I calculated that Catherine's fracture was almost certainly for the best.

There was one stroke of luck. I managed to break our coffee machine while I was descaling it. Reluctant to confess that, given the chain of events, I put the machine away in the cupboard under the kitchen counter but tilted it over cleverly so that when the cupboard was next opened it would fall out.

As philosophers often asked, "If a coffee machine falls from a cupboard, was it a sin?"

H

Most Tuesdays, lunchtimes were devoted to what was known as "rounds" in which each week one of us presented an interesting case to the other doctors in the department. This week, Oliver Michaels was presenting, and it pained me to admit he did an excellent job. As always, there were know-it-alls who wanted to get one over the speaker and demonstrate superior intellectual skills. These characters were found everywhere in medicine and were desperate to score points. That led to my Tenth Rule, which despite appearances wasn't just a variation on my fifth one:

BRIAN'S 10TH RULE — ALSO KNOWN AS THE STANDISH PARADOX

The more you think of yourself as a doctor, the less your opinion should be trusted.

The key take-home point was that the over-humble doctor was probably intellectually bereft and best avoided, while the one who had an overly high self-opinion was best limited to practise on rodents and single-celled organisms.

The lunchtime round ended, and the attendees made a beeline for the sandwiches. For reasons that have been lost in the mists of time, wealthy doctors always broke into a run for free sandwiches, as if they spent most of their lives at food banks or diving in the bins behind McDonald's restaurants. Equally unclear was how we'd reached a point where we had pharmaceutical representatives sponsoring meetings like this one for the honour of putting up little displays of why their blood pressure drug was better than the last one and giving us pens trumpeting Adalat slow release or something like that. It used to be called Adalat retard, but for reasons undefined the name was changed.

In typical hypocritical fashion, I grabbed a pen and a sandwich and drifted back to my office to avoid talking to any of my colleagues, who strangely interpreted my rudeness for wit, and who all apparently liked me, unaware I held most of them in low esteem.

H

On Friday, I finished at midday so I could meet Harvey at the rental house. Ever since his diagnosis, he'd been astonishingly well. I'd imagined him lurching from side effect to side effect from the medication, but other than making chicken taste metallic, he said there were no problems at all. Apart from fatigue, he felt remarkably well and hadn't had a single infection of any sort in the past two years. Harvey had become much more his old self, and I couldn't help reflecting on my patients in the early 1990s whose journey was so terrible.

All patients were important, but some left their marks on you forever.

HENRY AVERNS

We had had a young man of twenty-one with hemophilia, Neil, whom I recalled distinctly coming for a routine follow-up appointment and showing me an odd lesion in his mouth, which looked like candida, a yeast infection. He also had some skin lesions developing typical of an HIV infection, which was, of course, the diagnosis.

There was nothing in their training that helped doctors tell young patients that the medication they thought was saving them had become an executioner. It was even worse when doctors asked themselves if certain outcomes were predictable or avoidable.

Neil spent much of his last two years of life in one of our isolation rooms, with even more distressing infections, and severe weight loss to the point that when we lost him, he weighed ninety pounds. He left behind a wife and a daughter who had battled with Neil's illness and the stigma of AIDS in the early 1990s. I needed Harvey to do well. He was in my own mind some sort of redemption for the sins I perceived had been committed in the 1980s.

When I got to the rental house, Harvey was waiting in the driveway. He had a small tool like a cross between a knife and a saw that he said was for us to cut a hole in the wall. Harvey had arranged with the tenant for us to go in and do this. She told us she was now unable to walk at all, had meals delivered, and had arranged for a caregiver to come and wash her.

By this point, it was pretty clear where the scratching noise was. Harvey cut a small square, about five inches on each side at the chosen point, then prized out the wall. The smell was appalling, and we were staring at a dead rat. Harvey produced a pair of washing-up gloves and fished out the corpse, whereupon about a second later a rat shot out, crossed the room, and leaped onto the sofa. The immobile tenant jumped off the chair and dashed out of the apartment screaming.

Harvey grinned. "You're a bloody good doctor, Brian. I think you've cured her."

23

STDs and Murder

On Monday, we learned clinics were to be cancelled for the week. A full-scale investigation was taking place. Chris Abbott had been found dead in Operating Room 10 the previous morning. The initial opinion was death by suicide, but this was soon abandoned when Chris's fellow narcissist, Richard Headley, told the investigating police officer, Inspector McAlister, about a conversation he'd had on Friday evening with Abbott, who had described in detail what he'd been looking forward to the following day.

Chris's secretary knew his password, and thus the email invitation to a sexy nitrous oxide liaison with a female junior doctor was determined. The lethal hypoxic encounter was discovered by Sunday at lunchtime. By mid-afternoon, the hospital was closed to visitors and all surgeries were cancelled for the next few days. McAlister set up a command unit in the outpatient block and brought along his deputy, Olga Ivanov, to ensure we took the investigation seriously. Olga seemed particularly dour today, as if recently she'd failed to secure a job she'd applied for on a firing squad.

The female junior doctor who had set up the get-together was summoned on the Sunday morning and cautioned. She, of course, denied all knowledge of the incident but did admit she'd received a strange message from Dr. Abbott around lunchtime on Saturday, asking her to wear overalls later that day, which she'd ignored because she assumed he knew she was going to the Young Farmers Ball that evening.

We even had a news team outside the main doors covering the event, and a few times my phone rang from numbers I didn't recognize. I decided I'd head home an hour into Monday morning, but as I was leaving my office, Jeremiah Foch and his two sidekicks were walking in my direction. They were clearly in their element. Here was an opportunity to control and organize their workforce as never before. Sidekick number two presented me with a timetable, telling me I was to report to the outpatient clinic — somewhat ironically, the sexually transmitted disease unit — for an interview with the police inspector at midday.

I arrived ten minutes early and was made to wait a further fifteen while Headley's wife was being interviewed. She came out flushed and agitated and had obviously been crying. Pushing past me, she fled the outpatient block in a hurry. I was invited into the room and took a seat where a patient normally perched to the side of the desk, with the inspector positioned where a doctor would normally be. On the wall behind was a rack containing a range of informational leaflets on herpes, chlamydia, and safe sex. McAlister took a few basic details about my role in the hospital, then threw me completely by asking, "Where were you on Saturday afternoon?"

Inexplicably, I lost all power of thought and speech, then blurted, "I ... I'm not sure." I then calmed down a little and regained my composure somewhat. "I would've been at home. My wife can be my alibi."

"Och, and why do you need an alibi?" crooned the Glaswegian. "Is there something you want to get off your chest?"

"No ... I didn't kill him."

"Oh, so you believe this was a murder?"

By this time, I was almost convinced I looked guilty and was going to ask for a lawyer when the inspector changed tack.

"Who would've wanted Dr. Abbott dead?"

"Well, I guess he left a few women feeling a little aggrieved."

"Go on."

"I'm pretty sure he gave one of the junior doctors an STD."

"STD?"

I pointed at the board of leaflets. "Look behind you. One of those."

He briefly glanced at the leaflets. "And you know this how?"

I explained how I'd seen Chris at the other hospital, then hinted at spotting him being romantic with one of my junior doctors.

"Being romantic?"

"Having relations," I clarified.

"You mean shagging?"

I thought that was a little coarse for a professional, but nodded. I also told him about Chris's most recent partner's black eye and suggested that at his previous hospital he might have left other wounded victims.

"What about work colleagues here?" the inspector asked. "Anyone with a feud?"

I considered Headley and his wife's dalliances but held my tongue. A frisson of realization passed through me once again as I reflected on the past few years' events. I was haunted by Oliver Michaels's words when he'd spoken to me after the previous deaths: *Do you believe me now? The median life expectancy of a consultant has dropped again.*

Until recently I'd remained highly skeptical that the deaths were anything other than coincidental, but then I thought about our house fire and the potential electric shock from my office light. I decided to look for Oliver, but with the hospital effectively closed, he wasn't able to run a clinic, so I assumed he was staying at home.

Inspector McAlister terminated my interrogation abruptly. I felt I'd been a disappointment and was also conflicted about my decision not to mention Oliver Michaels's repetitive warnings that something was afoot in the hospital. Deep down, I was increasingly certain there was a large target on my back and that indeed a murderer was among us.

H

After a lot of speculation, I heard from my secretary that an arrest warrant had been issued for Oliver. Initially, I was shocked. He was a man who irritated me beyond redemption but didn't strike me as the sort of person who could take a life. I was highly doubtful he'd win a fight against any of my deceased colleagues. On the other hand, he was an unknown quantity — he lived alone and didn't socialize with his fellow doctors. In the end, I accepted that the sequence of events might be starting to make sense. Oliver had disappeared, his car was missing from his home, and the rumour was that his passport hadn't been found in a police search.

That suited me fine. If Oliver was trying to finish me off, the further away he was from me the better. I still changed the locks at home and arranged for a burglar alarm to be installed, though after the third day when we set it off yet again, we were already not arming it.

24

Morris Dancing

In lieu of what was going on at the hospital, I decided to take the week off. There was a series of summer events in Kilminster, so we went into town. Catherine was in a walking boot with partial weight bearing but had insisted on accompanying me. She had arranged for a hair wash and trim.

In the market square was a troupe of Morris dancers. I'd been harbouring a secret desire to be one of these ever since my last birthday. While not known for possessing any sort of innate rhythm, I was sure I could do the simple steps involved, which didn't seem to require much more than counting to four followed by a little jump. I thought perhaps that Morris dancing was an alternative to a midlife crisis.

Catherine didn't share my enthusiasm. She actually had the audacity to tell me I was lame. Even the children seemed to disapprove of my ambition. I did point out there was a cool after-dancing social culture involving beer and badinage. Catherine then correctly observed the paradox of my misanthropic nature and my newfound desire to socialize.

As I stood in the marketplace watching the dancers, Catherine left for her trim. The dancers were doing something that looked suspiciously like all their other capers. An old man, clearly in his nineties, was playing the accordion, and next to him was a young man, perhaps in his eighties, performing on a tambourine. I noticed that almost every dancer had a beard, and my father's warnings about facial hair came to mind.

To my absolute dismay, I saw Jeremiah Foch adorned in ribbons and bells. To my even greater dismay, as the dancers stepped toward one another clicking sticks, I glimpsed Jeremiah partnered with none other than my brother, Harvey. What a total bastard! How could Harvey have joined the Morris men and not invited me? I was literally speechless at his betrayal. But then again, upon reflection, it was a little lame, and perhaps I'd be better off choosing a different middle-aged hobby. I didn't fancy golf. The ridiculous outfits put me off as did almost everyone I'd ever met who played the game. Car restoration was also unappealing, since it required too much attention to detail. Perhaps I could take up wood-turning.

In a matter of minutes, I decided to agree that Morris dancing was a pathetic sign of an aging man. My ambition was like a damp bonfire that never quite got underway, and witnessing the medical unit manager leaping around like an idiot was the final straw.

Harvey and Jeremiah were rather annoyingly clapping their sticks and dinging the little bells on their garters as they pranced around to an old English folk song called "Tarry by the Maypole." Forty feet to my left, I looked up and saw the Estonian white van man who had been parking in my drive. He glared at me and started marching in my direction, so I hustled away from the market square and almost ran into Catherine. As we strolled back to the car, avoiding the market square, I said, "Your hair looks great. I really like the new style."

"It's the same. My hairdresser was unwell, so she cancelled."

25

Sexual Assault

The medical staff meeting in September was as dull as ever. There was a theme of negativity that gradually sucked the joy from the room. However, I was on a relative high, since I'd been invited to be an examiner for the College of Physicians.

Agenda: Medical Staff Meeting, Monday, September 11, 2000, 5:00 p.m.

Regrets: Daniel Collins.
Minutes of last meeting.
Review of outpatient space nursing needs.
Remediating failing doctors.
Increased parking fees.
Banning pharma reps from hospital.
Opening of the Pfizer-Lilly-Amgen Clinical Education Centre.
Revised annual leave rules.
Any other business.

A few years after becoming a doctor, a further set of exams were taken, probably the most challenging in a career. My recollection of that time was of many hours of study and anxiety, and I vowed I'd be firm but fair and a little less hands-on than the doctor who examined me.

I worked on these exams about three hours per night for several months.

Finally, the day of the exam arrived. I emptied my colon, peed myself dry, and sat in the waiting room to be called through. The format of the exam was one long case in which we had thirty minutes to perform a detailed assessment of a patient, then eight short cases, with about five minutes for each to convince the examiner we'd reached the level to become a member of the esteemed college.

My long case was a disaster. The patient was a diabetic with poor control. She'd been admitted a few days earlier and was believed to be perfect for the exam. But since being selected, she'd developed hospital-acquired diarrhea, and by the time she came to the exam, she was vaguely confused. It was impossible to obtain any reliable history, and when I attempted to examine her, she grabbed my arm with her right hand and smeared dysentery all over me. She even brushed it on my tie, at which point I backed off and elected to fabricate the rest of the history and exam.

The exam candidate had to present his or her findings to the examiner. Mine was Dr. Philip San Antonio, who had a national reputation for being a self-promoting narcissist, and who wore a navy blue polka-dot bow tie, with a yellow rose in his lapel at my exam. Throughout our session, he seemed fixated on the brown mark on my tie. Off the bat, he asked, "Did you hear a murmur?"

The answer for this question was always: "Yes, very quiet and benign." I felt I passed the long case because San Antonio smiled and guided me by the elbow to the next case.

The first short case was easy: "Look at these hands and make a diagnosis." It was a case of rheumatoid arthritis. *Easy*, I thought, and San Antonio smiled again. His teeth were the same colour as his trousers, which were an unusual shade of dark mustard yellow. One down, seven more to go.

The second case was to perform a neurological exam on legs. Easy again, I believed. I'd practised on Catherine for weeks. San Antonio seemed impressed. He was surreptitiously picking his nose, and I was certain he grabbed the curtain around the bed to discard the evidence.

The third case was to examine a face and make a "spot diagnosis" to show you could diagnose a disease from a patient's appearance. My brain went into a total state of failure like a blue screen on a computer that wouldn't reboot.

"What are you thinking?" San Antonio inquired, raising an eyebrow.

He's as ugly as sin, I was thinking. But thankfully no words came out. San Antonio put his hand behind my back to guide me to the next case, embarrassingly touching my buttocks as he dropped his arm to his side. I smiled understandingly.

The next case was a borderline pass, and the examiner, too, made a borderline pass.

Before I knew it, I was on the eighth short case. I wasn't confident whether I'd passed or failed. For the last cases, San Antonio had accidentally demonstrated full frottage, murmuring "You're doing great" in my ear as something firm, probably his stethoscope, rubbed my buttocks.

I left the exam rather hoping, indeed knowing, that his sexual gratification would translate into a clear pass. I suspected San Antonio must have eventually faced a complaint about his inability to understand personal space, but if that was what it took to jump that hurdle, I'd take it. This wasn't a time when one could complain about totally inappropriate behaviour and expect to remain a member of the club, though I was already wondering if this was indeed a club where I belonged.

Nothing was what it seemed. Or was it? Was our initial opinion usually the right one?

BRIAN'S NINTH RULE

A man walking alone in the woods is a pervert. A man with a dog is wholesome.

My ninth rule remained more of a hypothesis, since it failed frequently, yet it seemed that with revision it could evolve. The facts were inarguable. As soon as you saw a male alone in the woods, you knew he was up to no good. Add a black Labrador and the whole scene changed. It was the same in medicine. Certain visual clues reliably highlighted colleagues to avoid. For example, add a bow tie to any male physician and it was a neon sign flashing and declaring his conceit. I couldn't currently think of any physician who wore a bow tie whom I would have let loose on a guinea pig let alone a human. Similar snap judgments applied to Audis designed to look like racing cars, people who wore scrubs outside work, and individuals who sported goatees.

I did amend the last part. I should have said goatees in men. We had a wonderful matron who often saved a little porridge on her facial hair, but she was worth her weight in gold.

I was sure I could extend the dog-walk rule to patients, but try as I might, found it unreliable. That you couldn't look at a patient and make a snap judgment has stood the test of time.

The patient who seemed intelligent, say, a university lecturer, was usually incapable of listening, while at the same time he or she would sit there nodding to imply immense understanding. The patient who appeared uneducated would be the one who asked the best questions and grasped the concept of uncertainty.

The nurse who you thought would have a good foundation always overestimated her knowledge and became the most challenging patient. Then there was the super-friendly patient who started to call frequently, expecting an appointment tomorrow, and when not granted, used language more akin to a sailor's. Or the apparently grumpy patient who turned out to be only anxious and became a lifelong delight to see.

But thankfully, most patients were wonderful, and the seventy-two different types of consultation mainly brought joy or hope. Of course, occasionally, you came across vile human beings. You only had to stand outside any pub at closing time on a Friday to know that not everybody was a kind, gentle soul. And when on Friday night that drunken harridan in the gutter hurled the f-word or a bottle at her boyfriend, or Wayne, with the testosterone pecs and the shrunken testes, thumped some poor guy trying to catch a bus, why should we expect them to make perfect patients on Monday?

As has been said, "A bastard with cancer was still a bastard." And that was the amendment to my ninth rule.

H

On Friday, I was asking myself, *How do you get a couple who are living in your rental apartment without paying rent to leave, without the expense of going through the courts?* The answer was: *You get your brother, Harvey, to sit at the bottom of the stairs in the common entranceway wearing an orange gimp mask and a black PVC thong, reading* Guns and Ammo *magazine.*

I received an indignant phone call from the couple, which was quite audacious considering they were living rent-free, demanding Harvey be removed from the upstairs apartment. I assured them I'd tried hard and that he'd asked permission to invite a few friends to a party that weekend.

Harvey was correct. The couple departed the same evening.

26

Red Flags, Waiting Lists, and Hospital Managers

The hospital was now double-red-flagged. What that meant was we were" failing." And by a perverse process of ministry logic, it signalled a drop in resources at the very time we needed more. Our CEO, Grace Jones, had known her days were numbered and had suddenly left on sick leave, knowing that after the axe fell, she'd be better placed for her next CEO post at another district hospital. As I distractedly perused this month's agenda, I sighed heavily.

Agenda: Medical Staff Meeting, Monday, November 13, 2000, 5:00 p.m.

Regrets: Daniel Collins.
Minutes of last meeting.
Proposal to streamline specialty services.
Finance director update.
Junior doctor new educational style. Problem-based learning.
Wait time initiative and failed accreditation —
    hospital in red-light status.
New rules on ink colour for charts.
Any other business.

After the seeming departure of our CEO, Jeremiah Foch and his side-kicks had developed a rather authoritarian attitude and had started to take over the triage of my clinics. For example, a seventy-eight-year-old patient with a ten-year history of mild anemia replaced a twenty-year-old with possible new leukemia to bring our average wait time down to acceptable levels. Meanwhile, the drug and therapeutics committee had now announced that some of the antibiotic therapies available for immunosuppressed patients, in other words, my patients with HIV and leukemia, now had to be approved by a committee and were no longer eligible to be prescribed by me. This, I was told, could save us tens of thousands of pounds per year.

Since the committee met once every four weeks, it would be great luck if a patient developed his or her infection at the right time, especially as a general rule, waiting three weeks to treat pneumonia was usually suboptimal. A form was even created for me to complete to apply for the medication. I'd protested and appealed and had asked to have this issue added to this month's agenda.

Now, Richard Headley grinned. "A dead patient costs less."

In fact, that wasn't true. There was always another patent to move into that bed.

Out of fifteen staff members at our meeting, not one supported my appeal. This was something else never taught in medical school — that human beings would look at their shoes rather than speak up. My colleagues were all quite happy for my specialty to merge with the tertiary hospital if that meant their own units were safe.

Sensing victory, Jeremiah proposed a working group to explore moving the care of HIV and leukemia patients to Birmingham. I was considered too close to the issue to offer an unbiased view and wasn't allowed to join it. The group was to be headed by Richard Headley and would include a new endocrinologist who had started three weeks ago, along with Jeremiah, his sidekicks, and a patient representative. The last was to be Captain Arthur Brookes, who was one of the governors of the local private school. The belief was that he'd offer wisdom and impartiality. Brookes was a widower who now lived a slightly incontinent and confused life in a vast former vicarage called The Orchards. He wasn't my first choice to advocate for hemophiliac patients with HIV, since the nuances of the diagnosis would be lost on him. Undoubtedly, he would feel their predicament was God-given as a result of a lifestyle choice.

I threatened to go to the press. Patrick O'Donnell, the medical director, told me that sort of whistleblowing would only lead to my dismissal and that perhaps there were some advantages in calming down a little. He assured me that the changes wouldn't affect my salary, then said the awards committee was meeting soon and he'd heard I was "highly likely" to get a merit award that would mean a pensionable increase in salary for life.

That evening, Catherine and I were unanimous. "You have to decline the award if it's offered and write to the *Kilminster Journal* and tell them your concerns," she insisted.

In our whole marriage, I'd never heard my wife swear until that day.

She added, "I checked our bank balance, and we have enough to keep us going for three months while you look for a new job."

Recently, I'd noticed Catherine seemed to be feeling wealthy. She'd even started paying ridiculous prices for gourmet dog food, even though I pointed out that our own dog seemed to be able to survive on vomit and other dogs' feces.

The editor of the newspaper refused to publish. He was a petulant man born somewhere just outside Wetherby and was the Labour Party candidate for an upcoming by-election. Clearly, he'd been warned that the hemophilia story was too hot to handle, since he told me as much in a lily-livered, pathetic phone call.

"I'm under too much bloody stress," he complained in his ghastly Yorkshire accent. "Me chuffin' ferrets got sugar diabetes and me son's been done for shoplifting. I can't be doin' with any more stress."

I decided to get a patient group together, knowing I was swimming against the tide of opinion.

27

I Play Sherlock

I'd never felt so disenfranchised from my role, so I sought refuge in clinical encounters and tried to be rewarded by the joy of medicine, attempting extra-hard to listen, though my attention span continued to thwart me. One patient told me she felt I wasn't hearing her at all, and I had to admit to myself that, in fact, I was bidding on a banjo on eBay during her consultation.

Later, I was looking through the desk drawer in the clinic room when I came across a small hematology handbook with the name "Alisha Sharma" written on the inside page. Flicking through her book reminded me of the bad luck we'd faced in Kilminster Hospital.

When I was back in my office, I sat at my desk with a pen and began to list the deceased of the past few years. I added arrows and lines where there were connections, then appended a few other names where I saw links.

Eventually, I ended up with some names, and things became clearer to me. For Inspector McAlister, the Chris Abbott case was closed. To the inspector, Oliver Michaels was the only potential suspect. But were there others? So, as was my habit, I wrote out a detailed list:

MISSING, SUSPECT, OR DEAD

Kate Morgan

I initially thought Kate was drinking the night she died in the inferno of her car crash. Over the days following the accident, I wondered if she had a small stroke or some other illness. No police investigation ever took place. Could she have been drugged somehow? I was unable to meaningfully recollect the day she died. More telling, I could see no reason for anybody to wish her dead. She was quiet, kept her thoughts to herself, and was a family woman. Kate never picked fights and was pretty much the colleague we all wished for. I could find no motive, no clear method. Perhaps there was no foul play. Maybe I was already overthinking this. The police were certain her death wasn't one they needed to investigate.

Sally White

Neville, Sally's husband, had a cast-iron alibi, but I knew his life with Sally was miserable. She was a spiteful woman with few friends. The police weren't suspicious, but who ever died from a cassowary attack? Why was Inspector McAlister so happy to call this an accidental death? Who would want her dead? I added the word *not* to that sentence, too. Sally was a truly toxic woman who picked fights with managers and colleagues and was as loyal as a snake. Could Neville have planned for her to be murdered? That would need funding, and I doubt he was ever allowed any pocket money.

Who else would gain by the death of a cardiologist? Would Richard Headley be better off? I suspected yes. He would have a more lucrative practice and more personal power in the hospital … but enough to make him a killer? I figured he was already pretty well off. But he did always seem to be around when somebody died and never looked anything other than nonchalant about each death. Even Inspector McAlister would benefit in some respects because he could have the Leyland cypress fence removed without consequence.

Oliver Michaels

Oliver Michaels expressed disapproval at Sally White's behaviour several times over the years but was pretty judgmental about many of us, and again, it felt paradoxical that a man who was a lay preacher could commit the ultimate sin. Then again, he disappeared after the last death. The hospital rumour mill said he had a relative in Spain and he was already there. The police weren't particularly interested in searching for Oliver yet were paradoxically confident he was the chief suspect. Nobody formally declared him missing, which seemed somewhat ridiculous. He had no family and the hospital didn't ask for any sort of investigation. Oliver's clinics were simply cancelled. Maybe I should talk to Jeremiah and ask him if we should contact McAlister and encourage the police to actually look further, since at present the inspector seemed very unwilling to show any interest.

Was Oliver playing us all along and now disappeared before being discovered? On the other hand, over the years all the qualities that used to drive me bananas had somehow become more tolerable. And irritating as Oliver was, I couldn't really dislike him, provided he was in a different room, of course. Of the people listed, Oliver was the only one who hadn't at some point or other stabbed me in the back — an unfortunate metaphor, I reflected.

Colin Marks

I asked myself many times if it was conceivable that somebody could perform his own colonoscopy. Once again, the lack of a police investigation was a challenge. Was that a deliberate manipulation by Richard Headley when he completed the death certificate? None of us ever questioned him when he suggested we write that Colin had suffered a cardiac death. There was no doubt that Richard and Colin had a toxic relationship. There were rumours about Richard's wife and another consultant conducting an affair. I assumed she was doing that with Chris Abbott, but perhaps she spread her joy even further? Was this just hospital gossip? Didn't I see her the day of Colin's death? Could she be involved in it?

I added Richard's wife to my list and drew lines to link her to Karen Morgan and Sally White, along with an arrow from the latter's name to Colin's. I also added Mary Taylor. Her relationship with Colin had been terse from the start, yet hadn't she taken a long period of time off after he died? Was that grief or guilt? I tried to talk to her a few times but was rebuffed. I remembered Oliver Michaels telling me he saw Mary leaving the hospital the morning of Colin's death.

Chris Abbott

Chris left a trail of disappointed women and presumably a path of chlamydia in his wake. But he wasn't around when Karen Morgan and Sally White died. If Richard heard the gossip about his wife and already distrusted her, this would give him a motive. Headley also had the knowledge and probably the opportunity. My junior doctor, Olivia, was clearly keen to share her affection with Chris, but I got the sense she accepted the consequences of her dalliance, so I didn't feel she wanted to kill him.

Her relationship with Chris definitely seemed like a consensual one. So who else wished Chris dead? As I told McAlister, I got a sense of potential domestic abuse with his current partner and perhaps that was a pattern of behaviour giving a motive for others to murder him.

Barb Tomlinson

Barb's postmortem pretty much excluded her from any suspicion of foul play explaining her demise.

Alisha Sharma

I found myself writing Alisha's name again. There was something just beyond the reach of my mind. The best thing was to leave it and the thought would mature over the next day or so.

I didn't want to paint myself as some armchair detective. This whole deliberation on paper took me five minutes. I was aware I was unlikely to get far with this process. Inspector McAlister seemed involved in most of the cases, and I suspected he enjoyed the easy life. Our pathologist, Rashid Chopra, was another notoriously unimaginative and idle man whose postmortems were often limited in their investigative scope.

At that moment, my pager beeped. It was the lab. There was a problem with one of the blood assays and could I pop down? I left my doodling on the desk and headed to the lab a few doors away. We had a procedure for quality control to make sure our blood tests fell within an acceptable range of accuracy, and the control samples were pointing to an issue. When I got there, it was a simple fix. One of the reagents needed changing, and we were up and running within twenty minutes.

When I got back to my office, Headley was standing at my desk perusing my doodling. As was often the case, a huge grin split his face. "Hi, Sherlock! So, are you going to get us all in a room and announce the name of the killer? And what's this name here? My wife? Are you actually serious? Why would she be involved? She's five foot two and weighs about forty pounds. And look, my name's highlighted in fluorescent yellow. What does that mean?"

My lips were totally dry. I'd never been a convincing liar. My mouth opened and closed like a dying fish's.

Richard burst out laughing. "Brian, it's fine. I know about my wife. We've had an open marriage for at least five years. And yes, she did have a fling with Colin Marks, but I doubt Chris Abbott would've been her type however hard he tried. She seemed attracted to dissolute characters, so Chris was far too healthy for her! Look at me, after all. Anyway, Brian, I wouldn't leave this sort of thing on your desk. If there is a killer among us, which the police don't believe, then it was Oliver Michaels. I suspect at this very moment he's somewhere in Spain never to be seen again."

I had genuinely believed he was about to murder me. My hands were still trembling.

"And one more thing, Brian. Watch your back." With that, he turned and left my office, whistling a funeral march as he went.

I remained for a further twenty minutes unable to move. I was nervous about heading to my car alone and waited for a couple of people to leave the lab so I could walk with them.

28

Time for a New CEO

Grace Jones, our CEO, resigned. She actually didn't quit. She announced a prolonged leave for her unspecified sickness. This was a common strategy at that level because it exempted her from the failure of the hospital while leaving her ready to step into the same role in another failing hospital.

Jeremiah Foch was promoted to a new level of incompetence pending a new permanent appointment, though Kilminster Hospital was tainted. We were unlikely to get the cream of the crop. And, of course, the best managers chose to work outside the Health Service. The post was advertised, and the first time around nobody applied. On the second attempt, we got six applicants, including one who wrote from an open prison in Norfolk and another who apparently had a breakdown in his previous hospital, assaulting the chair of the League of Friends when she spilled his mug of tea on his scone, owing to her tremor.

The final short list included a middle manager from a local shoe shop, a woman who ran a home-delivery macaron company, Jeremiah, and a monk who had left his monastery three months earlier but who had a background in health care. This turned out to mean he'd taught a first-aid course to Boy Scouts fifteen years earlier.

Indeed, a fine field of candidates!

Because the hospital was now in emergency administrative measures, a policy was announced that no consultant staff members were eligible to sit on the interview committee other than Patrick O'Donnell, the medical director, whose ability to form relationships was robotic. Did I mention he was a neurologist? The interview committee consisted of the director of finance, Joyce Rush, who was perfectly affable and capable and who had avoided conflict for several years; Reverend Cyril Leahy, our increasingly confused previous chair, along with the current chair;

a patient representative, Meelis Kask, whom I knew nothing about; and Mark Stone, representing primary care.

My own preferred candidate before I set eyes on any of them was Mrs. Macaron, mainly because while I'd never in my life heard of a macaron, my two girls were impressed and found a photo of a purple thing sitting on a piece of black slate on the candidate's website. We hadn't seen her CV, but I assumed she had some previous health-care management experience in addition to her kitchen skills.

I did get an invitation from the chair of the hospital, Desmond Blackburn, retired chief of the Kilminster police, to meet the candidates the night before the interviews. This was to take place in the old consultants' dining room, which promised to be quite the event, since at least two-thirds of the medical staff had agreed to attend. Nurses weren't invited other than their director. No other groups essential to the function of the hospital were requested to attend.

The managers' desks, which were the original tables from the dining room, were pushed against one wall. Jeremiah Foch's primary sidekick had bought a box of Shiraz wine and was struggling to figure how to get the nozzle out at the bottom. If everybody chose wine, we'd each get half an ounce, I calculated. There was an urn of hot water, a choice of chamomile or peppermint teabags, and some powdered coffee. Nobody remembered to order cups or glasses, but the sidekick's sidekick found some paper cups near the water dispenser in the staff-and-relative canteen. I noted to myself that there was no paperwork involved when the cups were relocated to our soiree, which must have been quite a struggle and left the sidekick's clipboard hand a little twitchy.

The candidates were invited to mingle and did their best to look comfortable. I very much doubted that many of my colleagues would be gentle with them. Mark Stone was wearing a T-shirt that would have fitted a child and jeans rather than a suit. He stood talking to the patient representative, who kept gazing across at me. I'd seen him before but couldn't place him.

I managed to talk to Mrs. Macaron, who was delightful. Her niece had multiple sclerosis, as it turned out, but that was her only qualification for the role of CEO at our hospital. She'd retired from her first job as a receptionist at Kilminster Plumbers to establish a bed-and-breakfast at her farm. Mrs. Macaron had increasingly enjoyed catering and had set up her macaron business after one of her guests tried one two years earlier. I asked her why she'd applied for this job and she told me her husband had died quite unexpectedly and she no longer wished to run a bed-and-breakfast.

Mrs. Macaron believed she was too young to retire at fifty-three and still had a lot to offer. She'd brought with her twelve macarons in assorted pastels. There was nothing to dislike about her, but it was hard to imagine her controlling the ambition and treachery of the middle managers and the equally disloyal behaviour of the medical staff. It took a very special person to bring together so many unpleasant personalities, many of whom had forgotten the ultimate mission of the hospital: to care for people.

The shoe shop manager was a little out of her depth, too. She'd forgotten to do the most basic research, was unaware she'd applied for the CEO position, and though she was in her early thirties, dressed like a teenager. She was talking to one of Jeremiah's sidekicks, who politely pointed out they'd been in the same year at the local college of further education. I never got a chance to speak to her because she slipped out of the room, and I didn't see her again until three months later when I came across her in Footwear Fashion, where she sold me a pair of tan brogues.

The ex-monk was next on my list. I'd expected a godly man with a tonsure but instead conversed with a fellow with a comb-over and 1974-style yellow tinted glasses. There was a sheen of sweat slicked on his face, and a nose with the biggest blackheads I'd ever seen. He kept adjusting his genitals through his pocket as I tried to get even the vaguest sense this man was employable anywhere at all, let alone as a hospital CEO. Unfortunately, he was asked to leave halfway through the evening after a criminal check returned late in the day, raising concerns that weren't fully defined but were enough for him to make a hasty exit when our human resources manager whispered something in his ear.

Of course, everyone knew Jeremiah Foch. I was sure he had only one suit and a single shirt, which, as always, gaped at the navel and had his trademark dark patches under each armpit. Jeremiah had clearly reviewed the government's latest health-care goals, could quote every target, and had prepared fifty photocopied handouts setting out his analysis of each one, itemizing where we were and how we would arrive at paradise. I noticed him picking his ear, then inspecting whatever ended up on his finger, before reaching toward me with one of the handouts. I politely declined.

Everyone gradually filtered out of the dining room, leaving Jeremiah, his two sidekicks, Richard Headley, who had drunk the whole box of Shiraz, and me. The patient representative was at the far end finishing off any remaining refreshments. He even took half a macaron that Cyril Leahy had left on a paper plate and stuffed it into his mouth. When he turned, brushing orange pastel crumbs of meringue off his shirt, he scrutinized me again. Then, in a moment of terror, I recognized the white van man, now lurching toward me. I made a very swift exit, dashed along the corridor and was relieved to see that he didn't follow me.

After the meet-and-greet, I hurried to the basement to collect my laptop. Hospitals at night were always a little creepy. The pathology department was in darkness, though the on-call lab technician was in her office. She was going through a church music phase, and I heard "Abide with Me" being played by a colliery brass band.

I walked into my office and retrieved the laptop. Underneath it was the suspects list I'd been assembling. My eye darted to the last name — Alisha Sharma — and I suddenly knew exactly where I could find her.

29

Smells a Little Fusty

I must have known where I could locate Alisha Sharma ever since Catherine and I had bought our rental house. So, I left my laptop where it was and hurried to my car. Behind the passenger seat was the tool Harvey had employed to cut out the square in the rental basement. I didn't return to my office but went up to the management unit where my old office used to be. It was deserted. The only light was a dull green glow from the fire exit sign at each end of the corridor. I entered my old office and stood perfectly still. Complete silence. Should I turn the light on? Suddenly gripped by fear and anxiety, I decided not to. This was stupid, so I turned to leave, choosing to come back on the weekend with Harvey.

And then for the first time in my life I developed courage. I was going to carry through with this now. And if I was wrong, I could just deny any knowledge at all about the damage. I knelt behind the desk, which was still in the same spot as it had been when the office was mine. There was only one possible location. One wall had the corridor behind it. One was adjacent to the next office. One had a large window and a radiator beneath it. But the fourth wall was different. It abutted a newer wing of the hospital.

I crouched down and started sawing. Within two minutes, I'd cut out a square. My eyes adjusted, and from the light issuing in from the window, I could see well enough.

Tentatively, I tried to reach my hand into the hole, but the opening was too small and I had to enlarge it. It was now more like eight-by-eight-inches square. I reached in again and my hands touched something that seemed like a plastic bag. Tearing at it with my hands, I opened it a little. All I could sense was an irregular wooden joist. As I worked down, the wood changed direction and turned more into what appeared to be strands of wire. This wasn't what I'd expected.

I calmed down a little, my initial excitement and fear now becoming an impression of foolishness. I probed a little farther. Odd. What was this? Were those toenails? Complete panic and terror nearly engulfed me as I realized I'd just worked my way down a leg and foot. It made no sense. Surely, I'd expected this, yet the reality still seemed completely impossible. I withdrew my hand as if it were in the mouth of a wild animal, hyperventilated, even moaned weirdly. I sat there in front of the hole, rocking, trying to slow down my breathing.

Then there was a sound. I turned to look and saw something dark swing straight into my face, as if somebody was smashing a table into the front of my head. It was brutal, threw me about three feet, and left me lying on my side, dazed and confused. That was followed by a huge arm around my neck, constricting my breathing. Everything faded, not to black as I'd read in books but to bright white.

30

A Bridge Too Far

I had an intense pain in the side of my head, severe nausea, and was going to vomit. My hands were tied behind my back, and I was in the rear footwell of a large car. I sensed crusted blood around my ear and couldn't see the driver because my face was buried in the carpet, which smelled of wet dogs. Every time we went over a bump, I swore I heard reindeer bells.

Although I couldn't look up, I still felt the driver was peeping back at me as we shot along dark roads to a destination I already knew had only one outcome — Richard Headley. Could I talk to him? Would he listen? It was no surprise to me that Headley was a psychopath. A medical student could have made that diagnosis. Try as I might, I couldn't get my thoughts together. Why would Richard kill so many people? He was present or potentially present at every death and now was going to be committing mine.

Then I sobbed rather pathetically as I thought about Catherine and our children. Would they find my body? What would they do? Catherine had made steak-and-kidney pie for Friday night's supper. Who would eat it? Would she be annoyed with me? I pictured her sitting there with the whole pie on the table. We hadn't sold the rental house yet. What would happen to that? I hadn't even been invited to be a Morris dancer.

The reindeer bells kept on tinkling, and I gradually became a little more lucid. There wasn't enough light to see anything now, so I figured we must be on dark country roads. I was sure we'd driven for at least two hours. We were definitely a long way from Kilminster, and there was a thirty-minute period when we were on a motorway.

I tried to talk to Richard, but he merely turned up the volume until the music of Mike Oldfield was uncomfortably loud. That reminded me instantly of Karen Haythornthwaite, the unlucky girl who could have been a girlfriend of mine if she'd washed her underwear properly. I prayed to

God and promised that if I survived this ordeal, I'd get in touch with her, realizing I'd abandoned her rather harshly many years ago. Another of my resolutions was to spend more time with my mother, who must be so lonely. But I didn't have any more time for sentimental empty promises, because the car slowed down and parked under some yellow street lamps.

The driver's door opened and then closed. There was a little shuffling outside, and the rear door cracked at my foot end. I was expecting some clever quip from Headley. What I actually heard was Jeremiah Foch. I could now see under the lights and realized the tinkling noise was coming from his Morris bells in the footwell of the car. Even more disturbing, I understood that what I'd thought was wet dog was where my face pressed into the crotch of his Morris dancing trousers.

He roughly untied my hands, and I grabbed a bell and ribbon from the footwell. It was hardly the weapon of choice, but my plan was to make a run for it at the first opportunity. Jeremiah was colossal, and I doubted he could run more than a hundred feet before collapsing. He dragged me out of the vehicle, putting my right arm painfully behind my back in a vise-like grip. Hoisting my hand toward my neck so that I ended up standing by the car on tiptoe, he shoved me forward, and I saw we were at one end of a metal suspension bridge.

I was sure I'd seen this bridge before. There was nobody around. I guessed the time to be around midnight. He pushed me hard to the middle of the bridge. At no point did he say a word. In my dreams when I was the hero, I always spun around and thumped the villain. But in my panic, I was unable even to vaguely negotiate with this bad guy. Watching too many movies perhaps, I'd also expected a James Bond–like triumphant explanation of all his crimes and a final dramatic denouement. But Jeremiah was mute. He lifted me to the top of the railings just as car headlights came into view at the far end. Hastily, he shoved me over, and I believed I was falling to my death in the gorge below when once again everything turned white.

31

Ashes to Ashes

When I woke up, I thought I was floating on air. It was very cold and dark, but there was enough light to discern a vague set of shadows above me. A light shone down at me for a moment, then I remembered nothing more until I awoke to a hymn. "Abide with me" drifted to me from above. I tried to look up and distinguish what had happened. But opening my eyes only caused a torrent of sand to land on my face, stinging my eyes. I could barely see. I rubbed the dirt off and spat out an ashy taste from my mouth. When I glanced up again, another load hit my face, making me choke. Then I heard a few voices hurrying away.

I was still clutching the Morris bells, so I rang them to attract attention, but the noise was lost in the wind. A powerful light flashed down again from above, and I distinctly heard the word "Brian?" It was more a question and quite uncertain. Then I heard another voice say, "What the hell? Something moved down there. There's someone down there." The light flickered down again, but I was unable to shout. I was numb and wasn't sure I could rationalize what was happening. I just lay there about fifteen feet below the bridge, vaguely waving a pink ribbon.

Within twenty minutes, a blue light beamed above me, then powerful floodlights dazzled me, revealing the bridge was undergoing repairs and I'd landed on a safety net attached to a huge metal platform suspended under the bridge.

A rope was dropped down, but I was frozen to the spot and lacked the courage to let go of anything. It was at least another hour by the time a man in an orange jumpsuit descended toward me and attached a harness to my quaking body. I was unceremoniously hauled up to the bridge edge, and even then, I remained totally paralyzed with fear, or with hypothermia. As I flopped onto the asphalt of the bridge, the first person I saw was Richard Headley, grinning, as usual, inanely.

It turned out it was Richard who had called the police. A family had sneaked along at night to illegally dispose of their uncle, famed for his head of curly hair, who quite coincidentally had died in Kilminster Hospital and who bore a striking resemblance to the missing Oliver Michaels. They had run at the first sight of a blue light but were now standing at one end of the bridge, holding an empty urn, and were of no interest to Inspector McAlister, who had just turned up after a call from Headley, his close friend. Richard had followed Jeremiah to the bridge and seen the whole thing. Why hadn't he come to rescue me earlier? I'd have to ask him in due course. Olga Ivanov was there, too, her face in its normal angry repose, as if disappointed I hadn't perished.

"I thought you were a goner, Brian," Richard now told me. "I just saw you being thrown into the gorge. And then when the family came to sing a hymn, I actually thought perhaps they were in cahoots with Jeremiah."

It was already 7:30 a.m. I was sitting in somebody's car wrapped in what appeared to be tinfoil. An ambulance arrived to take me away, but I politely declined. Nevertheless, the foil was swapped for a red blanket and I was gently led to the ambulance doors. Then, before I knew it, I was stepping inside. When I argued further, the paramedics eventually realized that other than bruising I was quite capable of refusing their medical care. That settled, I waved at Richard Headley, who pulled up in his Audi and agreed to take me back to Kilminster.

In four hours, Jeremiah would be offered the CEO post, so I assumed he'd be at the hospital, since he had no idea Richard had witnessed my attempted murder. On the way back to town, Headley and I tried to make sense of the various deaths but were unable to.

McAlister and Headley were clearly excited to get there first. Of course, it was Headley in his Audi who drove fastest, but the inspector parked diagonally in front of the main hospital doors and "won" the race, having driven over some newly planted shrubs. Strangely, as we entered the hospital, Olga Ivanov was already there. I wasn't totally certain, but I thought there was the hint of a smile on her normally miserable face, as if crowing that weak British men had taken far too long to arrive.

The plan was to go and arrest Jeremiah, but McAlister said he needed a statement from me first. I was sure he would have preferred my case to be attempted suicide, since that would have been less effort for him. We agreed to meet in the cardiology offices.

When Richard and I settled in his office, he pulled out a black book from the shelf of old textbooks behind his desk, leaned toward me, and held it out. "Take a look, Brian. Alisha Sharma showed me her medical school yearbook when she was first appointed. After she disappeared, I kept it. She left absolutely everything behind when she departed."

Of course, Headley was unaware of what had happened in my old office, which ironically was about ten feet from the cardiology suite but a five-minute walk out of this building and back into the old part of the hospital. Somewhere behind Richard's desk was Alisha's body in a cavity where the old and new wings joined.

When McAlister arrived, he, Richard, and I entered the office where I'd first been attacked and asked Jeremiah's sidekicks to leave us for a while. They quickly grabbed their clipboards and departed. I closed the door and walked over to where there were four white file boxes in front of the hole I'd made, obviously put there by Jeremiah. Moving the boxes, I commanded, "Put your hand in there, Richard."

Headley actually did as I ordered. He knelt and reached into the hole, groping around, clearly unimpressed. I had a few seconds of self-doubt before he shouted, "Jesus fucking Christ, what the hell's this?"

"I'm pretty sure that's Alisha," I told him.

McAlister was thrilled and was desperate to look himself. He didn't have a flashlight but tried to peer through the hole in the wall, holding up his silver cigarette lighter. "I can't see a thing, but I'm buggered if I'm putting my hand in there. Shite, it smells disgusting."

The inspector got up, pulling himself up with the help of the desk, breathless with the minimal exertion. His excitement was evaporating as he realized he was going to have to follow up on all this. He'd originally planned to spend the day lying on his sofa watching the snooker championship. Sighing, he declared the whole office a crime scene, and we hung around for forty minutes until a young woman police constable arrived and let us go. She had the much-sought-after job of standing in the corridor until the crime scene team arrived at least another two hours later, by which time I'd finished telling my story to the inspector back in Richard's office, and he left, leaving Headley and me alone.

Richard picked up the yearbook and handed it to me. I worked through the pages and found nothing.

"Go to the *F* section," he urged.

Before I did that, I looked at the G's. There was Davy Garfield, who I'd trained with five years earlier. He'd decided to be a streaker at a rugby game in Cardiff and was suspended from work until the end of the six-month post. Before choosing medicine, he had completed a microbiology degree, and interestingly some blamed his suspension on the fact that he had also picked an argument with one of the professors over the safety of importing factor VIII harvested from paid prisoners in the United States. Davy was now a professor of orthopedics, which ruined my theory about specialty stereotypes.

There were only three students with a last name beginning with *F*. Two were female and the third was a pale, bespectacled fellow called Jeremy Fuchs. Add a hundred pounds and a large beard and I was eyeing Jeremiah. And who could blame him for changing that last name. Nobody would think twice about "Foch."

"Alisha recognized him immediately," Richard said. "He was thrown out in the fifth year after a couple of unexplained patient deaths. Apparently, nothing could be proven, but everybody knew he was involved. However, when he assaulted a house mate with a screwdriver, that was enough to remove him."

He glanced at me, and instead of smug indifference, I saw deep compassion and intelligence.

"No criminal case," Richard continued. "Everything brushed under the carpet. No investigation. Sound familiar? This is just another version of factor VIII. Keep the reputation of the medical school and the profession intact. Alisha told me that the last thing he ever said to her was that doctors would die for throwing him out of medical school."

"And Jeremiah's downstairs now being interviewed by the media," I said. "He thinks he's won. What about the others? Did he kill them, too?"

"Neville never believed his bird killed Sally. He told me he actually had a pipe-dream plan for it to happen, but the stork was too tame."

"Cassowary."

"Whatever. But Jerry had the opportunity and knew Neville was in the hospital. I suspect he made everything up as he went along. And to be honest, I think Neville was so relieved to be rid of Sally that he was happy to accept the story, however much he doubted it."

"What about Chris Abbott?" I asked.

"I think Jerry had the medical knowledge to do that, and didn't you notice how much the two of them butted heads at every one of our meetings? And we know Chris was lured down to the operating theatres with a promise of sex. He enjoyed the moral low ground and made me look like a saint!"

"But you said you thought Oliver Michaels killed Chris," I protested.

"Yes, well, I was second-guessing everything for a while. After all, Oliver did disappear on us. And to be honest, with Colin I still don't believe Jerry could have gotten a colonoscope *that* far up, so I thought it had to be someone with experience using a 'scope. And Oliver could be that person. He certainly disliked both Colin and Chris. Jerry knew you were beginning to get too close. I'm not sure our pathologist considered cyanide, but when Barb died, I wasn't convinced she choked on that chocolate. Don't forget our pathologist has the imagination of an ameba and has made an art of compressing an hour's work into ten minutes."

"Those chocolates were on my desk with a thank-you card from a patient," I said, realizing I'd escaped death at least four times. I thought about the house fire and knew I should speak to Catherine, who must be trying to decide whether to defrost a chicken for Sunday lunch that weekend. I had called her from Richard's car, but since then had been carried along by the events. I needed to get hold of her once more to ask her to collect me.

I dialled the number, but the call wasn't answered, causing me to tremble. I imagined her being bundled into Jeremiah's car or lying dead in the kitchen, a rack of never-to-be-eaten scones on the side. *I guess I could still eat them*, I mused.

"Why not change his name to Fochs?" Richard asked, breaking into my reverie.

"Fochs sounds worse than Foch," I replied. "I would've chosen Smith, though."

"No, not Fochs, Fochs."

I stared at him blankly.

"*F-O-X*. Fox."

"Aha, yes, indeed. I never thought of that. Let's go and ask him."

32

The Interviews

Inspector McAlister had gone off to the old dining room where the CEO interviews were to take place. He'd told Richard and me to remain in Headley's office. Initially, we obeyed, with Richard passing me a box of tissues to wipe away the remains of the cremated ashes off my face. The rain had turned them into a white cream, giving me the appearance of someone about to perform an Indigenous ceremony.

The interviews were well underway when I got there. Richard had decided to get us coffee and had gone off to the canteen. I could see the panel through the glass door of the interview room, and its members seemed animated other than Cyril Leahy, who was in a deep sleep. It was no coincidence that Mrs. Macaron was scheduled third, at exactly the same time as the coffee trolley was arranged. They hadn't even ordered the ginger nuts. Mrs. Macaron had already arrived and was sitting in the waiting room with a large white box on her lap containing sixteen mango-flavoured macarons, each with a piped green sprig of mint on top.

Sandra, the shoe lady, had decided, after all, to return for an interview, which was now over. She was sitting with Mrs. Macaron wearing a skirt about three inches below her crotch, with a spangled glitter ball for a top. Of course, I was later told, she was utterly clueless during her interview, knew nothing about health care, and had the intellectual curiosity of a stone. In short, almost a perfect candidate for the CEO of any hospital. Despite her age and ignorance, it was clear that some of the panel saw the potential to have a puppet whom they could manipulate to their own ends.

Meanwhile, Jeremiah was currently halfway through his interview, all bulging white belly and sagging crotch of him. Oddly, he'd removed his jacket and was obliviously wearing his light blue shirt with sweat patches spreading from armpit to belt buckle, with the addition of a little dark stain below each of his 44B breasts. He was holding a ring binder in which he'd placed his many proposals for Kilminster Hospital. Although he appeared even more dishevelled than normal, the panel couldn't doubt his knowledge and vision. At one point, Jeremiah glanced up just as Inspector McAlister peered through the glass door to the interview room.

Suddenly, Jeremiah leaped up, grabbed his chair, and charged at the three interviewers. He gripped Reverend Cyril Leahy around the throat with his left arm while waving the chair at the other interviewers, shuffling backward toward the door, and yelling for them to stay back. There was nothing to suggest any of them had any intention of doing otherwise. He backed through the door, the vicar with his feet six inches off the floor, urine dripping from his left ankle.

McAlister backed away as Jeremiah and Reverend Leahy crashed through the door. At the same time, I was in the waiting room, my face smeared grey with ashes. Jeremiah gaped at me in total horror, not because of my appearance but because he no doubt thought I was dead.

Jeremiah then hit a fire alarm, causing every door in the hospital to swing shut. With his other hand, he hurled the chair he was clutching across the waiting room, striking McAlister square in the face and leaving him dazed on the floor.

The vicar was thrown to the ground, and Jeremiah careered out of the waiting room and down the corridor toward the fire exit. Coming through the same door was Catherine, Harvey holding a brick, and Richard with coffee, who casually put one foot out, tripping the fugitive, who collapsed in a sweating heap of blubber and anger. Harvey chucked the brick at his face, and Jeremiah stopped squirming. He simply lay there. For a moment, I thought he was dead, and glanced at a yellow portable defibrillator on the wall.

"Brian, *you* might think Catherine's a great cook, but her bread's only good for one thing." He pointed at the brick, which turned out to be a whole wheat loaf with pumpkin seeds. Then he stared at Jeremiah. "And did you steel my underwear with the rainbow on the crotch?"

McAlister had recovered from his blow and had stumbled over to where we were all standing. "Rainbow-crotched skivvies? My God, I've seen that very pair of Kecks." And he quickly told us about the corpse in the holiday rental apartment but failed to clarify that he'd delegated that particular assignment owing to the cup semifinal.

Jeremiah slowly rose from the floor, looking utterly deranged. He made a step toward me, and I backed away. Then he turned to run toward the elevator bank just as the lift doors were opening and Nigel Robinson strolled out. "Oh, you guys, look a little sweaty. I wonder what you've been up to, nudge-nudge." He stopped as I slammed him in the face with the whole wheat loaf with pumpkin seeds. Actually, I didn't, but I really wish somebody had. Nigel needed urgent behavioural correction.

Jeremiah then made a last-ditch rush for the elevator, which now smelled of onions, followed by Richard and me, clutching the defibrillator. When the lift doors closed behind us, Jeremiah reached for Richard's throat, crushing him against the side wall where a poster offered support for employees who felt threatened in the workplace. Being short, weak, and cowardly, I merely watched. Then I realized what I needed to do. The elevator was ascending, so I charged up the defibrillator and seized the paddles, which I rammed onto Jeremiah's capacious behind, pressing the button. He let out a roar, turned toward me, and then froze, wheezing and clutching his chest before slumping to the floor. Richard just stood there and stared.

"Oh, shite, I think he's dead," I cried.

"Don't get any nearer. He's faking it."

"No, seriously, he's blue."

"What the fuck? Do we have to resuscitate him?"

"Hippocratic oath, mate."

"We never did that at my medical school."

Jeremiah was distinctly dead. Richard gave him mouth-to-mouth from eight inches away, while I offered cardiac massage with my left little finger. Well, we had to try.

The fire alarms were screaming. The elevator doors opened, and we saw two firefighters racing down the corridor, along with a paramedic.

Behind them, standing in the hospital foyer, I spotted two members of the interview panel, each holding a macaron.

33

Confession

With Jeremiah Foch dead, Inspector McAlister never got a face-to-face confession from him, but the police did discover his written testament of sorts for some of the murders. Here it is with a little editing.

Back in 1997, at one of our medical staff meetings, Margaret Crocker passed the plate containing one ginger nut biscuit to Karen Morgan with her usual ill grace. Karen didn't want a ginger nut biscuit, but she saw me sitting there staring at her. She could see I wanted the biscuit, and with some mildly cruel satisfaction, I expect, elected to eat it and savour it.

It was about ten minutes later that she began to feel the room spinning and a mild disorientation. Perhaps she wondered if this was one of her migraines and decided to get out of the room before she collapsed. She saw me following her. What she couldn't do was read my thoughts, which were more or less that a craftily designed plan to get Margaret Crocker removed from her post, preferably permanently, hopefully fatally, had failed. And failure always irritated me. I saw Karen run into Brian Standish, who said something to her, but she just pushed through the door to get to her car and home before she vomited. Then, as everyone knows, Karen pulled out of the hospital and managed to make it to the ring road before losing control of her car.

H

Let's revisit February 1998 now. Neville White cleaned his boots carefully and soaked a roll of barbed wire in a tub of antiseptic. He removed his socks, then went and stood outside for ten minutes before summoning the courage to lift the roll of wire and drop it onto his foot. Stifling a scream, he felt a rising dizziness and nausea, so he ended up lying on his side on the front lawn, whimpering.

Nigel had already completed the other part of his plan, which was to move Claudette, the cassowary and other unpredictable female in his life, into the emu pen before heading to the hospital. As he reached the hospital, he realized his plan was doomed to fail, since the cassowary was overly affectionate and he wasn't even sure Sally would enter the pen.

An hour and a half later, I arrived at the White farm, parked 200 yards up the road, and followed a public footpath to avoid being seen, before crossing over the field toward the farm. It was getting dark, and Sally's car wasn't back yet, so I settled into a cold waiting game behind a dilapidated greenhouse with several broken panes and the straggled remains of old tomato plants growing through the gaps.

I knew Neville would be stuck at the hospital for a few hours — he had ensured that by speaking to the manager in Emergency. Luckily, things were going to be slow in any case because there was a charity parachute jump by three members of the local committee for the Osteoporosis Society, and two of the parachutists had sustained vertebral compression fractures. The plan was simply to smash Sally over the head with the ten-inch metal bolt I was swinging in my right hand.

My hands were pretty numb by the time I saw car headlights coming up the drive. I watched as Sally parked in front of the garage and strode into the house. When I saw the kitchen light come on, I started to make my way to the door but bumped into the metal edge of a wheelbarrow containing some cut shrubs and a sickle placed on top. I enjoyed improvisation, so I put the bolt in my coat pocket and picked up the sickle.

A side door from the farmhouse opened, and I could see a figure putting on some boots. I could just about make out the shadow of Sally heading down to the animal enclosure. Keeping close to the orchard trees, I followed her, gripping the sickle to weigh its value as a weapon against the bolt. I'd researched the relative risks of different ways of murdering and sensibly felt that blood added another layer of effort afterward.

Two minutes later, Sally was by the pen, picking up a dustbin lid. I crept across the yard toward the pen, observing Sally inside the bird enclosure herding the emus in the direction of the door. For a moment, I noticed one of the emus turn and make an aggressive movement toward Sally, but then it followed the other emus. I was now at the gate. Sally was about to turn around. I swung the sickle to my side and quickly stepped toward her, at which point I received a blow to the shoulder from the dustbin lid.

She was coming at me now, had recognized me for sure. I swung the sickle at her loudly, hitting the dustbin lid again. But I could see she was unsure what to do next. She thrust the lid at me and screamed a tirade of inarticulate abuse. I stepped into the arc of her next swing and drove the sickle hard into her belly. She didn't even scream but let out an ugly moan and a long exhalation, then simply dropped. It was that easy.

I was pretty satisfied with the outcome and was already rehearsing how things could be more efficient next time. I felt no emotion. No guilt, no regret. I had a torch in my pocket and shone it at her face, which was as unappealing in death as it was at any of our meetings. I raised the beam and saw that the emus had come back out of their shed. Clearly, Sally hadn't locked the door properly.

Time to go. I retraced my route back to the car and headed home where I placed all my clothes in my wood-burning stove, then went upstairs for a long shower. I kept the sickle, my new favourite weapon. With Sally dead, wait times at the hospital would go up. With wait times rising, the CEO would eventually be gone and I could rise to where I always belonged — the top.

At no point did I consider this death would be blamed on a cassowary, but God worked in mysterious ways, and the combination of an uninterested police inspector and a failed plan by Neville still achieved the desired endpoint and left everybody satisfied, other than Sally, who was probably somewhat disgruntled.

H

Next, we go to April 1998. Much as I'd like to take credit for the demise of Colin Marks, I have to hand that honour to Mary Taylor. But what follows is what I imagine happened.

Colin and Mary managed to hide their affair with total success for three years. They perfected the illusion of Mary despising Colin for unspoken past sins. The stench of cigarettes and Scotch seemed to be no deterrent to Mary whose highly organized personality allowed the deceit to successfully continue. Her own husband suspected nothing, even when their child showed no sign of his Ghanaian genes. Her husband had spoken to the family doctor at one point and had been fully reassured that a Black man and a white woman could have a blond child, and in his innocence, her husband gave it no further thought.

Colin mentioned his blood loss to Mary, and they agreed that a colonoscopy in the early hours of the morning before the endoscopy suite opened would be possible. The plan was only to inspect the last twelve inches of bowel and then do a more definitive procedure. The plan also was not to use any sedation. Colin had performed enough procedures to know that just looking at the last part of the colon wasn't a big deal.

But plans didn't always pan out. At twelve inches, Mary saw some blood coming down from higher up, and they agreed, as he lay there with a black tube exiting his anus, and framed by his hairy buttocks, that perhaps she convert to a full colonoscopy. Mary inserted a small intravenous cannula and gave Colin a low dose of sedative to make the procedure more comfortable. Whereupon Colin started to ramble incoherently about his undying attraction for Richard Headley's wife, who was reputed to be generous with her affections. Unconcerned and unaware of his indiscretion, Colin slurred that he wanted more access to Theodore, Mary's blond son, whom Colin was sure was his own. The colonoscope was almost at the caecum, the very first part of his colon. She didn't even think about it, just shoved him, with the colonoscope still inserted, off the table. He cracked his head on the trolley holding the video screen as he fell.

Mary didn't bother to wipe off her prints, but she did move Colin's hands to the 'scope's controls before hurriedly exiting the hospital by one of the side doors, narrowly avoiding crashing into Oliver Michaels as she rushed to the car park.

She drove around town for thirty minutes, then returned, making sure to greet as many people as possible as she walked through the main foyer.

Then there was the ambassador's favourite chocolate. Barb Tomlinson died within sixty seconds of chewing the chocolate that I had heavily laced with cyanide. I wasn't present to witness the immediate results of my first attempt to murder Brian Standish, but I was at the scene within three minutes when there was a state of general alarm and panic. I spotted Estelle rushing off to find help. The corpse was left alone for about half a minute, plenty of time for me to grab a further chocolate and digitally insert it into the back of Barb's pharynx before Estelle returned with Brian and his irritating old bat of a secretary.

Fortunately for me, the cardiac arrest team got lost and upon their arrival was as incompetent as any team I've ever witnessed. The team did come to the conclusion that Barb was choking and made a couple of futile attempts to dislodge the obstruction. One of their members proposed a tracheotomy, but by then she'd been dead for a good twenty minutes, and even the meddling Brian suggested it was time to call it a day.

Despite the failure of the mission, I was paradoxically satisfied that I'd perfected another new technique of murder. As before, I felt not an ounce of regret for my victim but frustration that Brian had avoided his deserved fate. I was well aware that Brian was poking around Alisha Sharma's apartment in town and that it was only a matter of time before things were out of control. I'd tried to kill him twice, once with the house explosion and then with the switch wires he'd left exposed in his office. This second attempt was particularly disappointing because the electricians had been in the department and represented an ideal group to blame for the planned death.

🄷

Lastly, in September 2000, my intention was never to hurt Oliver Michaels, but I had no choice. The plan was meticulous: an assignation with Chris Abbott, the embodiment of narcissism, who was too arrogant to have any insight that this might not be about sex. It was too easy.

Abbott, I'd learned, had read that sex on nitrous oxide gave one the best orgasm ever. I engineered a bogus email to Chris from a junior doctor with come-to-bed eyes, urging him to meet up to try this.

It was Saturday. The operating rooms were abandoned. It was boringly easy. Abbott did exactly as instructed, waiting in the anesthetic room near Operating Room 10 at the far end of the corridor and never used on weekends. As arranged in the email, he climbed onto the trolley and kept the lights off to avoid detection, The plan was that she'd creep up in the dark and offer him a mask of nitrous oxide before carrying out the lurid acts fully described in the email.

What was to decline? This was right up Chris's street. One could detect his anticipation as the door swished open and he heard steps walking up to the bed. He fingered his black eye mask excitedly and grinned widely as the anesthetic was placed over his face, but after sixty seconds of nitrous oxide, turned up above eight percent to make a hypoxic mixture, he became drowsy. Then sevoflurane was added to the mixture. He struggled for a few seconds before sinking into a sleep from which he'd never awake. As soon as he was under, I set up an intravenous line containing a prepared mixture of propofol potassium and vecuronium and started the infusion that would create the tableau of physician suicide.

This really was the perfect murder.

The challenge was that Oliver Michaels was watching right outside the door and was unable to disguise his shock at being caught red-handed. I can still recall our conversation.

"Oh, hello, Oliver, what are you up to down here? Secretly wishing you were a surgeon?"

"I … I'm doing an urgent bronchoscopy and was just trying to locate the 'scope," stammered Oliver as he backed away, patently aware that was the weakest of lies.

"I'm pretty sure it's in here," I said, pushing open the double doors into the recovery suite and grabbing a chest drain, then quickly peeling off the packaging.

"That's a chest drain. My bronchoscope is in a *rrrr*." At least there was one final Welsh rolling of the *r*, but I'll never know what he would have said because Oliver was impaled through the throat by a size twelve chest drain, a metal skewer about twice the thickness of a knitting needle. He staggered back, clutching at his throat, making gurgling sounds before collapsing to the floor in the corridor, twitching a few times before lying still, a gentle trickle of dark blood oozing from the neck wound.

"You've known all along, you interfering Welsh git. You could've just butted out, but now …"

The words were never heard by Oliver, of course. There was surprisingly little blood, but an inconvenient corpse. This was where psychopathy was valuable, because I felt nothing. No guilt, no anxiety. Perhaps some irritation that the evening would take a while longer.

Lifting the body onto a gurney took a surprisingly long time. But attaching a blue paper hat, mask, and a sheet up to the neck made this seem like a living patient who had been wheeled out of the operating room. It was Saturday evening. We passed two visitors and one surgical trainee, none of whom even glanced up as we headed to the mortuary.

There were no cameras and just one key code unchanged for seven years. And then it was a matter of exchanging the corpse. What luck! In the third drawer from the right, two down from the top, was the body of a patient seen two days earlier who was a close enough match. Oliver found himself lying in a drawer with a new tag on his toe and a signed certificate already on file to allow him a visit to the crematorium on Monday.

Meanwhile, I hauled Oliver's "double" onto the gurney, and once again passed the plausibility test as I wheeled him off toward the car park.

Nobody noticed the body being unceremoniously lugged into the back of a Mitsubishi Shogun.

The following morning, Sunday, the vacation rental owner was very happy to avoid commission fees and tax. She'd agreed to a cash price from the guy who had emailed asking to spend a week in an isolated cottage on the edge of the Forest of Dean, promising to leave the money in the bread bin.

34

Early Retirement

In the end, I had only had half a career when I decided quite spontaneously one morning that my days at Kilminster Hospital were over, and it was time to move on.

I discussed this with the family over shepherd's pie that evening and tempted them with promises of exotic travel and adventure. The children were of an age when measured reflection was still not a concept. Oddly, as I look back now, that was still the case a decade later. So, I handed in my notice with no new job to go to. That same evening, we opened an atlas and decided where our adventure would begin.

Over the weekend, I drove to work to clear out my office. Fleming Wing was empty other than a man cleaning the floor with a giant polishing machine. I heard it getting louder as he passed my office. Then the sound stopped. I sensed somebody standing in the doorway. When I looked up, I froze: Meelis Kask, the white van man. I had nowhere to go.

"I can emptying your bin?" he asked. "And I sorry I parking in your house."

Putting down the paper knife I was clutching, I indicated the waste bin, which was already overflowing. He handed me a black bin bag and said, in perfect English, "A thousand irreplaceable doctors have retired and been replaced." Then he took the pile of rubbish and in a grim voice added," I'll be back," in his best Terminator impression.

What a lovely man, I mused as I gazed at the box of junk I'd accumulated over a career. The room was full of things I hadn't been able to throw away: the snow globe from Tenerife given to me by my secretary, Tina, before her brief affair with Richard Headley, which led to an acrimonious divorce; the picture of Kilminster Cathedral painted by Edith Samuel given to me when her husband, Arthur, died after a six-year battle with leukemia; the tankard from Neil Stacey, who died in 1989, but engraved it before his death; a shelf of textbooks, all out of date and of no value; thousands of saved journal articles never consulted again; and several years of agendas.

I boxed them all up and wheeled them out to the car on an unused patient gurney. When I arrived home, I took them around to the back and created a giant bonfire. I felt no regret as I watched the books and files burning. I did have to grab a garden fork and shift the books around a few times, since they stubbornly refused to burn, but after three hours I was left with a large pile of grey smoking ash. For anybody considering a change of career, I can fully recommend the act of *irreversibility by conflagration*, which helps one to commit to a course of action.

There was a staff meeting that night, but I felt I could miss it. I did glance at the agenda, which said:

Medical Staff Meeting Agenda

Apologies: none.
In lieu of our meeting, we invite you to a special event to celebrate Dr. Brian Standish. Daniel Collins will lead the tribute.

35

My Last Day

It was my final day the following morning, a Tuesday. I didn't want to be seen leaving, so I sat in my chair for the last time and remembered the hundreds of patients with blood disorders who had died despite the best that was available at the time. I was sure I recalled every one of them. I thought about the patients with hemophilia who had died of AIDS or were still living with HIV and hepatitis C, and who had received no compensation for themselves or for their families, no clear explanation, and no justice.

I had no clear plans what to do next. My future was a blank page. The hospital had already advertised for my replacement. I didn't envy anybody starting a career in health care. The layers of bureaucracy that had seemed so awful when I started were a hundred times worse.

And I thought about my colleagues who had died in so many ways, and particularly of Oliver Michaels, who had disappeared the night Chris Abbott was slain. It was conjectured that Oliver had committed suicide. His body was never found.

Inspector McAlister believed Oliver's body had been exchanged for a patient in the mortuary and that his ashes had been dumped on me the night on the bridge. Until the inspector told me, I was unaware of my intimate relationship with my halitotic colleague. My hair had recently developed a tendency to curl.

I thought about my Rules of Medicine, knowing I'd struggled to come up with my original vision of the ten. I'd never even worked out Brian's First Rule. In fact, upon reflection, they really needed a little work. Who would have thought it so difficult to come up with ten simple rules? Perhaps I could start on those next week and have another bash at writing *Kathmandu*, my children's book.

When I walked to the hospital foyer for the last time, I headed to the exit past the League of Friends Café. I was cut off by a woman I hadn't seen in a few years, with a little girl of about five. Momentarily shocked, I stared as I recalled this same girl alone and frightened in a Nightingale ward so many years earlier.

"Hi, Doc. I've dyed my hair. It's me, Amanda. I'm just down visiting my sister in Kilminster. I'm still in remission. Bet you never imagined I'd have a baby? I'm pretty sure you told me I'd be infertile."

She noticed me gawking at the little girl. "This is my daughter, Rebecca. I named her after my sister." Her voice cracked, and tears welled in her eyes. "I just needed to catch you before you left."

When she reached in for a hug, I clutched her tightly. For the first time since the death of the little girl fifteen years earlier, I believed I could think of her without wanting to cry. I finally understood and could now write Brian's First Rule.

Brian's Rules of Medicine

FIRST RULE:

It only takes one patient to make the job worthwhile.

SECOND RULE:

Learn to enjoy saying "I don't know." It's not a sign of weakness.

THIRD RULE:

It's lower than you think.

FOURTH RULE:

If you earn more than twice the average income of a doctor, you'll end up divorced and with the average income again.

FOURTH RULE ADDENDUM:

If you're dumb enough to get to the fourth rule, you're highly likely to fail a second marriage and your ultimate value will be down to twenty-five percent from where you started.

FIFTH RULE:

The more certainty you hear from your doctors, the more likely they're talking garbage.

SIXTH RULE:

You can find joy in your career, your family, your hobby, or something else, but you can't have more than three. Choose carefully.

SEVENTH RULE:

When you set yourself up as a hero, expect vomit on your shoe.

EIGHTH RULE:

When a couple at a dinner party tell you they're having great sex, they're having none.

NINTH RULE:

A man walking alone in the woods is a pervert. A man with a dog is wholesome.

NINTH RULE ADDENDUM:

A bastard with cancer is still a bastard.

TENTH RULE (ALSO KNOWN AS THE STANDISH PARADOX):

The more you think of yourself as a doctor, the less I trust your opinion.

Author's Note

This is a work of fiction, but there are strands of truth throughout the book. I'll start with the usual disclaimer — the characters in this novel are fictional. However, every hospital around the world will share the same spectrum of humanity. It's thus inevitable that every hospital will have a philanderer, a narcissist, and doctors touched by the greed of the pharmaceutical industry. If you recognize characters, I insist that isn't my fault, but that of the human condition and the selection criteria when choosing new medical students.

There are almost certainly anachronistic errors in this book, though I've tried to avoid them. If the reader finds them, please accept them for what they are and don't tell me. I only enjoy positive feedback.

Throughout the story, there's the theme of what's often referred to as the "contaminated blood scandal." Again, I don't in any way set myself up as an expert. I make no apology for mentioning this in the book. In fact, it was what led me to despair about how seemingly good people can dissemble and lie, and feel it's a metaphor for the arrogance and corruption that exists in unlikely parts of the medical profession. And I also believe it's perhaps one of the most terrible insights into failure at every level in the delivery of health care. Thankfully, we still have a majority of our doctors and nurses who possess the qualities we wish for in our carers, but the events related to the infection of thousands of patients remain a terrible lesson.

Every year for the past thirty years, I've discussed the contaminated blood scandal with students and trainees and estimate that over ninety percent of the time this is news to them. That, of course, leaves me thoroughly depressed. If I were the dean of a medical school, I'd show new students the BBC *Panorama* program *Contaminated Blood: The Search for the Truth* in their first few weeks and ask them to reflect on the contents. Maybe encourage them to ask some questions such as:

- Why in some countries were custodial sentences handed out for those who shared responsibility for the events, while in the United Kingdom accountability was somewhat vague?
- Why did the Scottish pursue a different policy from other countries? How could they have interpreted the same data differently?
- Were there commercial pressures affecting decisions made at the time?
- How could patients receive infected factor VIII and not be informed of the risks and properly consented?
- Are we benefiting from hindsight?

Remember that in the early 1980s there were many uncertainties about the cause of AIDS, and some very influential individuals denied an infectious cause. The natural history wasn't well known, and given a choice between effective treatment for severe life-threatening complications and the quantitatively unknown possibility of AIDS, the prevailing medical opinion was to go ahead and treat.

So perhaps it was less clear than we believe — it was far from apparent what caused AIDS until the discovery of the virus. Perhaps we should balance the devastating impact of hemophilia and the life-threatening nature of the disease with the lifesaving development of factor VIII. Or perhaps not. My personal interpretation is that patients died, families were torn apart, and many cases were entirely avoidable.

These are just a few questions I've asked myself throughout my career. I'm not an expert. I'm not a hematologist. But I am a physician and have cared for patients with HIV and hepatitis C acquired from contaminated blood. I've sat with dying patients and asked these questions.

If you're prepared to be shocked, find the documentary *Factor 8: The Arkansas Prison Blood Scandal*. It's hard to locate. If you wish to learn more about this from those personally affected by the scandal, then I recommend a website that's probably the best resource for U.K.-related information: factor8scandal.uk/jason-evans. Jason Evans is an impressive and humbling man who's driven the process leading to the announcement of the Infected Blood Inquiry by Theresa May in July 2017. Some of the proceedings from the inquiry are available on YouTube. There are many other resources available for those who wish to read the whole story, but Jason's site is a good place to start.

Of course, narcissists and sociopaths exist everywhere. Every organization has the same spectrum of damaged and damaging humans. We'll never solve that. And, of course, it's true that the characteristics of these individuals help them make their way to the top in academia and business. In the novel, the phone call in the night about a medico-legal case is based on a true event.

And it's also true that the pharmaceutical industry has a history of unethical behaviour that undermines the faith of all but the most naive. There are many books about this subject, but one I found particularly readable as an initial primer to understand quite how corrupt the industry can be is Marcia Angell's *The Truth About Drug Companies*.

A particular personal dislike mentioned in the book is the concept of the key opinion leader (KOL), who are either:

- Amazing individuals who have intellectual prowess and have sacrificed much to become experts in their fields through research, teaching, and exceptional clinical practice.
- Self-serving individuals who have been involved in numerous drug-sponsored trials that have generated six-figure sums for the individuals and their departments and who can't possibly have the same clinical experience as average clinicians in communities, because they spend so much time flying around telling doctors how to practise.

There's a reason the pharma industry calls them KOLs: they're paid to spread the word. My rhetorical question is whether a conflict-of-interest disclosure before each talk effectively removes the conflict of interest. I suggest it doesn't.

The murders in the book are ridiculous. I understand that. I think it's likely that a cassowary would be hard to rear, and to cover up a murder in that way would be somewhat challenging. I suspect cyanide poisoning doesn't really seem like choking on a chocolate. I urge the reader to suspend belief for these. But the death of a child from asthma, with a frightened middle-grade doctor in the middle of the night nervous to seek help, was real in the 1980s. I truly hope this is no longer the case.

All health-care professionals deal with loss on a daily basis, and inevitably there are times when reflection after the event raises questions on how decisions and events unfolded. This is unavoidable. But the culture of fear of calling for help is entirely avoidable, and nearly forty years on from the events described, this remains an ongoing risk. There were huge faults with the culture of medicine at the time the book is set, and the impossibility of challenging this remains to this day.

I've spent too many hours of my life in medical staff meetings. Across the globe these are terrible. I've slept through most of them, so my recollections may, in fact, be dreams not reality.

I apologize to all hospital managers. I've clearly exaggerated their abilities. I seek their forgiveness.

I thank Harvey, who is real, for his frankness about being gay and living with HIV and for his enduring friendship.

Finally, I wish to pay tribute to the patients and families of the victims of the factor VIII scandal. Nothing I write can come close to understanding their experiences, but on a personal note, I've been touched by the events mentioned in this book and share their despair. The horror and stigma of AIDS in the 1980s and 1990s are hard to describe. You don't need the internet to be one of the vile humans who lob fire bombs at houses, graffiti the walls of hemophiliacs, and phone families with abuse in the middle of the night. Some things never seem to change.